The Unforgotten Prayer

Danny Rittman

iUniverse, Inc.
Bloomington

The Unforgotten Prayer

iUniverse books may be ordered through booksellers or by contacting:

iUniverse
1663 Liberty Drive
Bloomington, IN 47403
www.iuniverse.com
1-800-Authors (1-800-288-4677)

ISBN: 978-1-4502-9115-6 (sc)
ISBN: 978-1-4502-9116-3 (dj)
ISBN: 978-1-4502-9117-0 (ebook)

Library of Congress Control Number: 2011901690

Printed in the United States of America

iUniverse rev. date: 02/01/2011

To all the victims of the Holocaust for whom no one said Kaddish.

A man must descend very low to find the force to rise again.
— Hasidic saying

Introduction

THIS IS MY STORY – my life from the horrors of war and slaughter to the travails of change and atonement. For much of my life – far too much of it – I lived in fear that my past would catch up to me. I hid my beliefs and prejudices and walked among the gentle, unsuspecting people of a small town in rural Massachusetts. I lived a lie. I am, or was, an affront to the human race – an embodiment of madness, atrocity, cruelty and horror.

I had to remind myself constantly as to what to say and how to act and how to keep so much to myself. I had to lock myself out of life and live a maddening existence of deception, though I was once young and intelligent and capable of giving much to the world.

I had to remind myself how to behave, react and interact with those around me. I could not choose my friends, neighbors or the people I associated with. I could not express my desires and thoughts. I could not do what I wanted to do. I was locked inside my own prison without the ability to make any contribution, as I used to do – during the war and before it.

Most people seek to live lives that express their beliefs and selves. I could never do that – at least not until long after the war. Friends and neighbors? I shunned them. Social groups and religious organizations? I shunned them as well. Often I thought it better to turn myself in or die, one way or another, just to get everything over with.

That all changed one day – a miraculous day when a young

child came into my life and helped me back into life and towards reappraisal and a quest for atonement.

That young child was Jewish.

And I am a former SS officer.

Building an Empire

I T WAS NOT EASY to rebuild an empire out of a defeated and failing country after the First World War. I knew that the only reason that our party – the National Socialists, or Nazis – came to power was Germany's desperate condition. A once proud country laid low, its government and economy in ruins. No one would opt for a fanatical government under normal circumstances.

We felt these dire circumstances presented us with a wondrous opportunity, a once in a lifetime chance. And we took it. I say "we" because I joined the Nazi Party in 1932 at the age of twenty-two. I believed the Party was the only way to save Germany.

We went for it with all of our might, with all of our cunning. We used all means to win control over our nation. We used bribery, extortion, and even murder. Everything was Kosher to win my political battles. Funny – I loved to use this word "Kosher" with great sarcasm. I've just never told this to anyone lately.

Very early in the game we realized we needed to find a convincing explanation for our country's chaotic politics and catastrophic depression. We had to find something or someone to blame. We had to find an outlet for the unfocused fear and hatred in people. We planned our approach carefully, looking into every aspect of it. The answer lay with something that was engrained in many Germans anyway – anti-Semitism.

We started with propaganda directed at the masses. Any disappointment, any bad news, we blamed on the Jews. The people were ready for this. They were unemployed, bitter and full of anger that needed to be discharged on something or someone. Imagine millions of people without work, without money and barely eking out livings. The banks were badgering them about mortgage payments. What lenders there were charged exorbitant interest. People walked the streets with neither purpose nor hope. They came to despise the bungling governments that came and went without resolving the nation's woes.

Most recalled a time when government had brought them hope for the future and pride in their nation. We promised to bring that back. Germans were eager to hear our message – and to believe it with all their hearts as well.

The Jews were rich and educated. Everyone knew they dealt ably with money and wielded influence everywhere. This was done on the backs of earnest Germans. Those banks and lenders that exploited people? Jews, of course. The rest of them were doctors, attorneys, accountants and engineers. They lived well while Germans struggled to get by.

Everyone already mistrusted, disliked or hated the Jews. It all went back to the Middle Ages and the plagues and blaming those deemed responsible for Jesus' death. Much of it had gone into dormancy as modern times came and pushed rural folklore out of the minds of urban and progressive people. All we had to do was reawaken it. And with high office, we could do just that.

Channeling anger at times like those back then was a pleasant task. A concerted campaign to blame the Jews for the problems of the 1930s led to laws directed against them. The people accepted this readily – even joyfully. They wanted to hit, they wanted to break, and they wanted to feel relief from a decade of fear.

The Party gave them what they wanted.

We made the Jews a target – in time, a *legal* target – for hatred, abuse and murder. Enemies of the state, the bane of the Fatherland, revolting sub-humans, thieves, liars and the like. We became free to do anything we wanted. We took away the Jews' livelihoods, money and eventually their rights as citizens and human beings. It worked out better than we had imagined. The openings improved the lot of many Germans.

The rule of law? You forget the times.

We used their money and others' as well to rearm the military, which had been unjustly shorn of its might by the Versailles Treaty after the First World War. Germany without military might was unthinkable. The two things had gone together since the time of Frederick the Great. A weak military had added to the people's sense of powerlessness and emptiness. A restored one renewed their sense of grandeur and purpose.

Revenge against France was a duty we all strove for. We found many of the old generals too timid and resistant to the Party's goals. So we found more pliant ones to take their place. We looked for people that yearned for a restored empire. Men who would not hesitate to take bold steps once assured from on high by the Party. We gave them arms and purpose and they gave us victory and empire.

We began with Czechoslovakia, Poland and France then swallowed most of Europe – more than Charlemagne, Louis XIV, or Napoleon had ever realized. In every conquered land, we sought out the Jews there. Then we struck into Russia and enacted the same program. The Jewish problem was everywhere and a solution was needed to resolve the matter once and for all.

Yes, rounding them up and transporting them to the camps was expensive and a considerable part of the budget, but the enormity of the problem and the nearness of the solution made it worthwhile. Besides, Jews could be used in forced labor in war-related production. Industry thrived and so did the war effort. Our visionary ministers and dutiful officials wrenched every ounce of work from them until they were no longer of any use.

Yes, it was not always a pretty sight. I admit that now. But it was an ironic justice that those who had prospered from our toil were now our unpaid laborers. I discovered that some government officials charged factories for a steady supply of Jews. Some well-placed *Reichsmarks* here or there would bring in a fresh truckload of laborers. It all meant sense according to their accounting books.

Policing the matter was not high on our priorities, unless it led to labor shortages somewhere in our war industries.

The nation's economy was booming, our armies were on the march, and the extermination of the Jews was proceeding. As with any success, opposition soon emerges. That's simply the way of things. The SS, once Hitler's elite bodyguard, took on broader responsibilities. SS officers were carefully selected to perform their sensitive and vital work of maintaining the safety of the German people. Later the SS was charged with seeing that the Final Solution was carried through. Their numbers grew markedly and their work was done professionally.

I served proudly in the SS.

Against all predictions, Germany became an Empire again.

The Fall of an Empire,
Plan O Is Initiated

THE EXHILARATION OF VICTORY was overwhelming. It tapped into our souls and found a deeply-ingrained joy in national greatness – a joy, I would argue, not confined to us Germans. Exhilaration is wonderful but it can be blinding too. Our advances into Russia stalled and retreat followed. It took two years to realize that the reversals weren't temporary.

It was not a matter of numbers and economic output. To this day I am convinced that had we planned our war better and avoided a handful of miscalculations in Russia and elsewhere, we would be masters of Europe – if not more. We had many casualties in the Russian expanses and we had to fall back. Then the United States entered the war against us. This was a turning point – and not a good one.

It was as though a sorcerer had waved his magic wand and our luck left us. We started to lose battles. In the sea, land and even in the air. What we had once thought was ours by right of birth or through conquest, the British, Americans and Russians were taking – slowly and inexorably. I reluctantly rethought the course of the war, Germany's future and my own future as well.

At this point, Plan O was created.

Plan O was born while I was on leave in Bavaria, at the estate of an old friend, during Christmas time in 1944. After a dinner with friends, most of them back from the fronts, my girlfriend Alena and I went out to the balcony to enjoy the fresh alpine air, cold though it was. We hugged each other quietly as we looked out on the dark mountains, as the moonlight gently illuminated its silent peaks. The stately evergreens cast immense shadows upon the valley below and the pine scent filled us.

"The war is hard on you, darling," Alena whispered as she held my hand. "It is etched in your face now.... We should spend more time here."

"You're right, of course ... but I have my duty. Should I fail in that ... the Fatherland...."

I released a long sigh.

"Dear ... when will this war end?"

I was taken aback. We all thought about the question but did not want to ask it.

"I really do not know," I answered quietly. "We need to consolidate, gather our might once more...."

I was still under the spell of the Party.

"Who is going to win the war?"

The implicit uncertainty made me think I had heard her wrong, but the concern in her eyes made it clear. I had never allowed the thought of defeat to be considered. I was alarmed, but I soon calmed.

Her question was a legitimate one – one entertained in the army, I had heard indirectly, though not in the SS. She innocently asked the inevitable question that should be asked during any war – what if we lose?

I did not answer. After everyone went to sleep, I sat on the balcony and watched the bright moon track across the Bavarian sky. Arrogance prevented us from even considering the possibility of defeat, but I had to ponder the outcome. After Stalingrad and Kursk and Normandy, I had to ask, what if we lose?

If captured by the British or Americans, I would be given fair treatment. But not if I were captured by the Russians. We had mercilessly killed them by the millions and could expect nothing but retribution.

I thought about the inevitable discovery of our sordid work in the East: the concentration camps, the killing of millions of people including children and elderly, and other actions. Those things would not go away quietly. Our actions will excite outrage and prosecution – or revenge. We had crossed a line that could not be excused as merely part of war. People will be put on trial and executed. There was no doubt of that.

A moment of panic struck me and my heart raced. *This will bring no good*, I thought. I forced myself to calm down. There is no need to panic. Entertaining doubt had allowed that. That was it, I was sure.

We will win this war and complete our plans for the Jews and other undesirable people.

Lapses into fading certainties did not last. I had to plan rationally. In the event of imminent defeat, we would be ready. We will have a plan, an escape plan – a carefully thought out plan. I'll cautiously bring it up at our next meetings.

How shall I call this plan?

What does it matter what the plan is named? Just give it to experts – our generals. They will perfect it. Somehow I wanted to choose the plan's name and my imagination explored various ideas and ruminations.

The enemy will have to surround us ... like hunters closing in on the hunted – a circle. I smelled the strong pine scent and closed my eyes to savor it. I smiled as an idea came to me. We'll trick them. The letter "O" will be its symbol. An "O" symbolizes a circle – encirclement. If surrounded, we will break out of the "O."

Plan O....

The idea of the circle allowed me to think things through. We will have to find a way to escape this circle of doom. We'll have to be more clever than our enemies. I'll start to design this plan when I am back from leave. Not everyone can know of it; that can only cause problems and maybe even betrayals. My mind went into high gear. Almost everyone involved with the plan's design must be killed.

My mind fixed on the letter "O." It came to mean my survival, life – a new life.

Plan O

ONLY A FEW TOP Party members and SS officers knew of Plan O. Each person had his own escape plan according to location and time. Most of us knew nothing of the others' routes or identities. My Berlin adjutant, Hauptsturmführer Otto Kassell, was chosen by myself based on his fierce loyalty to the SS. Only he and I will have to execute my part.

His loyalty to me will be unrequited: after initiating the plan he will die, as he freely chose. Such were the mindsets of many in those days.

Plan O will help us escape to various parts of the globe, with each figure having choice as to his destination. I preferred a prosperous country, a place where I could live well. The jungles of Paraguay were not for me. I will become a retired Swiss businessman without family. I will live alone. My identity and appearance will be completely changed. I will take along enough funds to live well for the rest of my life – thanks to the pre-war gold bullion we had placed in Swiss banks. Better that we had it than the Russians.

And that's how it was.

Over a period of just a few months we created and refined the Plan. Every step was thoroughly thought out and set up for the right moment – when darkness fell on the Reich. My confidante and I would initiate the Plan at the designated time and place. After completing the Plan I felt relaxed, for I knew I would escape the hand of justice – or worse, the hand of the Russians.

Soon enough, the time arrived.

A New Man, A New Life

O TTO KASSELL'S FOREHEAD SWEATED profusely as we sat in a heavily-fortified underground bunker listening to the ominous sounds of the Russian army nearing Berlin. Kassell was a stout fellow with a thin mustache beneath a prominent nose. His eyes were surrounded with thick circles that gave him an overall porcine look. But he was my devoted adjutant and trustworthy. He knew Plan O as well as anyone.

With us were several high-ranking Party officials. Not Göbbels or Himmler, but some influential figures whose capture would be highly prized by Stalin. I was not so august as the propaganda minister of the head of the SS, nonetheless my capture would mean my death as I was involved in certain loathsome events, as you shall see. You've heard of them, no doubt. You may also have heard them denied. However, I assure you they happened. I played a role in some of them.

As the explosions from Russian artillery rounds got closer they changed from dull booms to fearsome cracks. We pondered the end of our Reich. They had won – at least for the moment, we thought. I looked about in frustration – and with occasional stabs of despair. But Germany history is as long as it is proud. Many of our noble leaders were not appreciated in their day.

Our greatness would be gone in a few days, perhaps by morning. The good we thought we had done would be pushed aside by the victors; we all knew that is the nature of historical writing. History would not see anything honorable about a quest to free Germany and the world from the stranglehold of Jews. Indeed, the history of our Reich would be written by Jews, and by those sympathetic to them.

I thank God that the history was not written by victorious Germans that our crimes have come to light.

"It is time, sir," I heard Kassell say.

I wrestled with fear and doubt and quickly turned towards him.

"Are you out of your mind?!"

I wanted to shout at him but I stopped myself. I was lost in dark reflections and in need of coaxing to come out of them. To his credit, he insisted. Kassell was coldly rational to my occasional fits of emotion – and that is why I selected him.

"There is a plan we need to execute."

Kassell stressed every word and in the panicky atmosphere of the bunker, he sounded severe. The dreaded moment had arrived. I shook my head and opened my eyes. He stood in front of me, motioning towards an adjacent conference room where great objectives for the Reich had once been formed.

"We need to ... discuss matters," Kassell insisted.

I had instructed him to see to it that there was no vacillation on my part. It seems so cold and cruel now, but that was how we thought and acted.

Some of the others there looked on at us briefly, probably thinking we had some last-minute words to have – perhaps a suicide pact. I assure you, there were many of those in those desperate final days. Whatever they thought, they did not show any expression. Years of military training were not lost and there was no emotion on their faces. They simply stood by and awaited their fate.

"Yes, we have to discuss matters," I repeated.

I looked at the officials around us. Many were dedicated Party members and SS officers with whom I had endeavored to build an eternal Reich. I would never see them again, I thought.

No time for sentimentality. Leave everything behind – Alena, family, home....

I did not want to go ahead. Maybe there will be good news. The darkest hour was just before dawn, Göbbels had told us. The Führer had worked miracles before.

No, we had to act. We had discussed in our preparation the likelihood of second thoughts and repeatedly noted the need for determined action. We had to calmly execute the plan and act like soldiers, like German soldiers.

I clicked my heels and saluted, as a well-trained soldier would – one who had served Wilhelm, Friedrich, Moltke, and of course Adolf Hitler. With that motion, I was ready to go ahead.

We entered the conference room and scarcely noted the maps with large red arrows closing in on Berlin. Kassell calmly sat across the large table from me. He was reserved and calculating. No emotion crossed his face. His steely blue eyes seemed never to blink.

"This is our last conversation in your current identity."

I nodded.

"After you exit this ... this tomb, your life will have ended. No loved ones, no home."

The protocols of Plan O required a final briefing. He seemed to expect a response from me, but I gave none. It all held true for him as well, though in a different way. He will commit suicide immediately to further limit knowledge of Plan O.

"Sir, you are certain you will proceed...."

These words – part question, part command – were not according to procedure.

I had to acknowledge the initiation. Only with my assent would we move forward. I touched the tip of my hat.

"Yes, let us proceed ... by all means."

I looked at Kassell as my last connection to this world – to the Reich. He had been with me intermittently since the rise of the SS in the late thirties. He had been my personal assistant in Berlin whenever I came back from my work to the east.

"Very well, sir.... I will need the key from you."

Our keys had been sewn inside our black SS tunics. I took my small army knife, slit open the concealed pocket and handed him the silver key that opened the heavy steel door in the conference room. The room had been the place of many discussions and I allowed myself a moment of amusement to think that no one had ever used it until this day or even knew what was behind it.

Kassell used his strength to push open the door, revealing a short hallway. At its end lay another door, which I'd have to open myself after I closed the first one behind me. Only after the first door was locked, could I open the second one.

"Thank you, Hauptsturmführer Kassell," I said in an official tone.

Kassell silently handed me the key then shook my hand before stiffening to a salute and smartly exclaiming, "Heil Hitler!"

His words reverberated in the hallway. I wondered how many others near us were saying the same thing before shooting themselves or taking cyanide. I further wondered how many other would deny they had ever given that salute.

I stood in front of the door and stared at it. *So normal*, I thought. But nothing ahead of me would be normal.

Soon enough, a skilled plastic surgeon would rework my face. My expressions, features, hair, lips and nose would all be changed. My eyes will be reshaped. Wrinkles will be added. My mouth will open and close differently and a new hairline will be constructed. The surgeon's discretion will be relied upon, not my personal preferences. He and his fellow surgeons had been carefully selected for medical expertise and loyalty to the Reich.

The doctor will stay with me for several weeks in a secure place. The bunker's unknown compartment had been stored with food and water for at least five weeks. Almost no one even knew about it. But the SS knew things – and Kassell had told me of it. It fit perfectly for me.

When my surgery was over and my new countenance had formed, I'll depart for Switzerland to complete my recovery. A car will be waiting for the doctor, but of course the car will explode shortly thereafter, thereby reducing the numbers of adepts.

I'll later travel to the United States of America as a retired Swiss businessman – a man of means thanks to some stolen wealth. I chose to live in a small town in the state of Massachusetts, near an enchanting lake. Webster – a dignified name, don't you think? There I'll live quietly and peacefully for the rest of my life. With the gold in my Swiss account, I can live away from the chaos of the post-Nazi world.

Ahhh.... Plan O was masterful.

I took a deep breath and closed the first door behind me, turning on a light above the empty hallway. I slowly walked to the second door, my boots clicking noisily with every step. The red lever would soon detonate a charge in the conference room and seal off the chamber. After pulling it, I had only one minute to enter the second door and close it firmly behind me.

A red bulb lit up above the lever as I pulled it. A timer had been activated and I marched towards the second door. I turned the key in a counterclockwise manner and opened the door. The handle was cold to the touch and I wondered what that portended. A bright light illuminated the entire chamber. I entered and closed the door behind me. A moment later, the charge detonated. The boom reverberated until giving way to the familiar sound of Russian artillery pounding Berlin into rubble.

with people, simple tasks were difficult. With the help of language records, I learned English and within a few months I managed on my own. I hired a local French-Canadian man to assist me with household purchases and within a short time my little home was nicely furnished.

My bedroom was on the second floor and had a balcony on which I could view the stars sparkling in the night skies. There was a large living room, a country-style kitchen and two other rooms that remained empty. I replaced the large windows with smaller ones as I felt a need to limit my exposure.

I bought several books about the Fatherland and the National Socialist Party – ones printed in Germany before the war. Naturally American publishers churned out books on the same subjects, but they were filled with lies that the Jews had concocted. I carefully hid my old books but brought them out when I felt homesick and weary of what I saw as the absurd lies swirling all around the United States.

My neighbors came to know me – to the extent they did – as a middle-aged man who kept to himself. For months I lived completely detached from the outside world, and I liked it. I had only the idle conversations of the citizens of Webster – the weather, a new shop now and then, and the sports teams in Boston, which I pretended to have a little interest in. Only rarely did I even ask someone's name. Only rarely did I divulge mine.

I occasionally heard talk of the gruesome discoveries when the allied forces entered the camps in Poland. I expected that. When someone expressed astonishment about such camps, I simply nodded in feigned agreement. That was to be expected in a country so far from the Reich and so deluded by its enemies, I thought. But these parochialism were the price I had to pay to live my new life.

I purchased a radio to give me some idea of the events of the world. It was a Grundig – a German company founded shortly after the defeat that was supposed to be emblematic of the new nation.

The reports I heard angered me. Germany was humiliated – enduring looting, debasement, and foreign occupation. There were even negro soldiers there. The Nuremberg trials were going on then.

They constituted an immense disgrace for the principles of law and the honor of the entire world. Many of our great leaders were prosecuted and condemned to death.

Well, I thought with sadness, this is the fate of a defeated nation. They take everything away from it and of course claim that our morals were warped and inhuman so they can humiliate and steal from us. Every night I listened in silent rage, until at last I threw the radio against the wall. As I looked at some of the pieces, I noticed that my Grundig had been built in Nuremberg.

That night was tortuous. The world was all wrong, I thought with great bitterness. If the world could see what I had seen, everything would be different. They would see the honor and decency embodied in the swastika and the SS lightning bolts – both of which I had been fiercely proud of.

At times I did not want to endure life among such lies. To hear on a daily basis all the ill-informed gossip about Germany and the war filled me with rage. Many nights I sat alone with my thoughts. No surgeon could ever replace what I had known with all my heart to be true. I decided, for reasons of my own sanity, to further reduce my contacts. It had to be so.

Years passed. I accepted the world's hatred of National Socialism. No one was willing to see the Jews for what they were. Worse, I discovered that the US was increasingly under their control. You could see it in the news as Jews were being elected to Congress and rising to prominent positions in industry. One day, I hoped then, someone would bring the world to its senses – as Adolf Hitler had done in Germany and much of Europe. I was only one man. I could never do it alone. The Führer had done it alone, but I was not he. Anyway, I was weary from the years and the long war. I had to finish my life calmly and quietly here.

After replacing a broken tube, I started to listen to my Grundig again. The war became old news and the country became more interested in the postwar affluence. My daily routine was serene and disciplined. I enjoyed the countryside and the seclusion it afforded. In

1953, I received my American citizenship and was even quite happy about it. Not because I held American citizenship high; because my plan had unfolded so seamlessly.

Decades had gone by and Webster had changed in the prosperous and restless years after the war. New people came in and the quaint hamlet lost its rustic simplicity. One day, the Rosenbergs arrived. It seemed a disgusting event then, but it changed my entire life and led to my atonement.

Jews

IDISCOVERED THEIR PRESENCE accidentally.

One day, during an early morning walk, I learned that a new house was going to be built. To my dismay the location was uncomfortably close to me – less than two hundred meters. Later I learned that most of the land in the area belonged to a prominent Webster family which had long kept it undeveloped but which now was selling tracts at prices greatly elevated since the war. I stopped near the site and looked on. *A large home*, I thought, as I saw a generous area marked by small flags. *So it will also have a large yard*.

"Good morning – the name is Elliot. How are you?"

I turned around and saw a young man, probably twenty-four or so, extending his hand to me. He was tall, thin, with dark hair. His attire was splendidly coordinated and crisply pressed.

He's either a perfectionist or has an obsessive-compulsive wife.

He was outgoing and like most Americans of the time, very polite.

"Kraus is my name."

I smiled at the young guy.

Why had I responded in such a friendly manner? Perhaps the human soul can only stand so much isolation and grumpiness.

"Johann Kraus.... I've lived in that house for quite a few years now," I added as I pointed down the lane.

"Nice meeting you, Johann," he replied with a smile of genuine warmth. "We've lived in Worcester for the last ten years but always wanted to move farther out into the country." He turned to the construction site and beamed proudly. "We saved for many years to build our dream home. Here we can have a family."

I nodded, understanding his excitement and thinking for an instant of my own plan to get here.

"Well, good for you ... and good luck."

I then turned to walk away. As instantly as my openness had come, it also vanished. I'd had enough interaction for now and I wanted to finish my walk and go home. I had lunch every day at two o'clock and today would be no different – regardless of the changes to the "neighborhood."

"I hear an accent in your speech," he said as I headed off. "Where are you from?"

Observant fellow....

"Switzerland. I used to live in Zurich but decided to retire here."

"Never been there, but I hear it's beautiful."

"Yes, it is. Quite cold in the winter. That is why I like it here – similar weather," I explained.

"Is your family in Switzerland?"

His friendliness had become curiosity – and that was unwelcome.

"I lost my family in the war," I said with no expression or further explanation. "I am alone in the world now."

I smiled bitterly as I thought of just how I had lost my family.

"Oh, I am so sorry to hear that."

His face expressed sadness but skillfully returned to a measure of cheerfulness.

"Well, now you will have us. You are always welcome at our humble home once it is finished."

If he would just know who I am, he would not make such a generous offer.

I gingerly shook his hand again.

"Thank you. I truly appreciate your kindness."

"Oh, by the way. We just had a baby boy two days ago – I'm a father!"

His eyes sparkled with a pride someone like me could not feel.

"Congratulations – and continued good luck."

I smiled to him, but now as a way to convey an ending to our chat.

They're probably a nice young family. Well, maybe it will become more alive around here now.

"Enjoy your day," I wished him as I returned to my walk.

Then he added some parting words that blindsided me. His words made the order and safety of my life verge on collapse.

"In our tradition, when a baby is born we say *Mazal Tov*, which means 'good luck.' "

As his face lit up, mine must surely have darkened.

"His name is Samuel!"

I tried to say something but words escaped me, though fear and other long-suppressed emotions presented themselves.

A Jew.... This must be my punishment.

"Nice...." I eventually managed to mumble. "I am tired now ... and I need to go home."

"A good day to you, Johann."

He waved a farewell to me then turned to greet the builder, who had arrived with an armful of blueprints for his consideration.

I knew that many Jewish refugees had come to America after the war, but that was in Boston and New York. Not here in Webster.

Your future means a return to my past. You've ruined my life with your mere presence. I thought I had escaped many things – war, prosecution, prison – but most of all I thought I had escaped Jews. But now Jews are building their home near mine – and adding to their family with ... what was it? Samuel?

Should I move elsewhere? Should I simply never speak to them?

I felt confused, unable to think straight. I felt undermined.

No need to panic. This is a free country based on individual rights. Every person is entitled to choose his friends and associates. Moving away suddenly might cause suspicion to fall on me. I'll just have to be careful and not show my true opinions about these people. Filthy Jews! I want nothing to do with them. If we were back in Germany in better times … well, there'd be a notice on their house – Achtung Juden.

Events conspire to toy with people. This time it was my turn to be toyed with. I felt like the world was exacting revenge upon me. Things were not going as planned.

I determined never to go near the Rosenberg home.

A few days later, on a tranquil summer evening, there came a knock at the door.

That Jew stood there and with him was a woman holding a baby. She was short, plump and dressed in simple clothes. She had dark brown eyes accented by a light amount of makeup. Every detail of their faces and attire and demeanor seemed to shriek out their race.

More ill fortune descending on me. An entire family of Jews is on my doorstep and there is nothing I can do about it.

Despite the many intervening years, images of my past returned to me within seconds. They had not gone away. They were deep within me. I wanted to shout to my soldiers to take them away.

They should not be here. They should be in their ghetto, awaiting deportation and….

Anger and frustration caused me to quake, but I controlled myself.

This is not the war. I am not in Germany. I am in America – a free country.

The Jews stood there and watched me in my discomfort. I was sure they enjoyed it.

"Are you alright, Mr Kraus?" asked Father Jew. He looked concerned … concerned with my health.

Now they inquire about my well-being.

I took a deep breath and controlled myself.

"Oh, yes. I apologize. I got a bit chilly in the night air."

I managed a half-smile. My security depended on my ability to hide my opinions and thoughts. My freedom and indeed my very life depended on cunning in this regard. I stood there hoping they had just come to say hello and would leave, but alas after some uncomfortable moments it became clear they hoped to be invited in.

Will I have to socialize with ... Untermenschen?

"Please come in ... and please excuse the foibles of an elderly pensioner. Do come in and have a seat. Would you like some tea?"

"We don't want to impose. We can always come another time," the Jew said as he sensed my discomfort. "I would like you to meet my wife and son," he said proudly.

"My name is Anne, and it's my pleasure to meet you," she said smiling brightly.

She had a pretty face. Many female Jews are attractive but that doesn't change their sinister nature.

"Oh, our home was just completed last week," the Jewess continued. "We are now in the laborious process of moving in. We'll be close to done by tomorrow. It's gorgeous, as is the whole area – but you know that, of course."

It is amazing how the Jews shrewdly took over the world.

Although Webster did not have many Jews, I noticed through the radio and papers that Jews were taking many prominent positions in Boston and its spreading suburban areas. They were considered full citizens and could do anything they want.

They've invaded my own home.

"Yes, Webster is lovely – and changing. Ah, the little one. What is his name? I'm sorry ... I forgot it – my age...."

Can they see my contempt?

"This is little Samuel. We came to invite you to the Brit Mila ceremony, which will be next Friday. Elliot told me that you are retired ... and by yourself. We would like you to be at our family gathering. We are neighbors now – and good neighbors are like family."

I almost gagged. First, the ceremony and then to suggest that I'm part of their family. I sat down breathing heavily. They noticed my unease and rushed to help. I had to make a great effort not to shout at them to get out of my house.

"Elliot, please get him a glass of water."

The Jewess made sure that I was sitting comfortably as her husband brought water. They both had worried expressions.

"Oh, please do not mind me. I worked in the yard all day and simply need a little rest."

I sat there awhile, organizing my thoughts as they studied my face for further signs of illness.

"I'm fine now."

These Jews seemed genuinely concerned with me. And hadn't they invited me to their gathering? They knew I wasn't one of them, yet.... I couldn't reconcile this with everything I held about their race. I despised these Jews. They and their offspring. During the war I helped round them up – to get rid of them like cockroaches. I saw in them a glimmer of ... of what? Humanity?

"I am a bit lonely out here ... Yes, I'd like to attend your son's ceremony."

Why did I say that? Maybe, I wanted to learn their ways. Maybe I wanted to better know their machinations to protect myself. I didn't know just then.

Their faces brightened.

"Do you know what the Brit Mila ceremony is?" the Jew husband asked me.

I meekly shook my head.

"The Bible calls for every baby boy to go through a ceremony called Brit Mila on the eighth day after birth. In this procedure a rabbi performs a circumcision – the removal of the foreskin. This is called 'Abraham Brit' and it symbolizes the boy's entrance into this world as a Jew."

He paused for a moment then continued.

"Our great ancestor, Abraham, performed the first Brit, conveying the covenant between us and the Lord. That is why we perform the same ceremony with every newborn boy."

I was disgusted to hear their revolting ways. They looked at me awaiting a response.

"Very nice. I did not know that," I said with feigned interest.

Obviously, the Jews had won World War Two, I thought. They managed to survive our efforts and become even more powerful. They misrepresented our policies and used them to ruin our homeland and extend their influence in Europe and America. A formidable enemy. I determined to study their ways in order to find their weaknesses. When the right time came I could use the information against them. This time, we would win and the world would be rid of them.

"Wonderful," the Jew said joyfully. "The ceremony will be at our home on Friday at ten am. Would you like me to come and pick you up?"

I waved my hand to say that a ride would not be necessary.

"I'll be there at ten."

"Look at little Samuel," whispered the Jewess. "So beautiful...."

I stood and neared the mother and child. The baby Jew slept calmly in his mother's arms as though there was nothing else in the world. His face was alabaster-like. His tiny hand gently clutched his mother's finger.

A Jewish baby....

I remembered what we did with the babies. They were no good for work so we separated them from their mothers and threw them, alive, into mass graves. Our orders were not to hold a baby more than a few seconds. We were not allowed to look, smell or touch them more than was necessary for their extermination. This prevented developing emotions towards them and interfering with the operation.

I looked at little Samuel – then chills came. I started to shake again, though not from anger or frustration.

An innocent baby in his mother's arms ... holding her finger.

I wanted that moment to last – to understand it.

"Sweet little Samuel," I said as I turned back to my chair.

I did not want them to see me like this.

"Friday – ten in the morning."

I was glad they did not notice my stress.

They left me with my thoughts – and memories. I sat their breathing in the fresh night air that came in from the open window.

The Jews whom I strove to annihilate now want my friendship. I cannot tell them who I am, I cannot tell them what I think, I cannot tell them anything.

I am a Swiss pensioner.

Brit Mila

FRIDAY MORNING CAME SOON enough.

I thought that the whole thing was crazy and it was taking a toll on me. Old ideas arose from my soul and did battle with other parts of me. For the past few days, I was wondering if I had been having a nightmare or perhaps even a nervous breakdown. Day after day passed without a decision.

Well, you have been in tougher situations. Remember your escape out of Poland? The Soviet T-34s were less than a kilometer away. At least, your enemy here is more civilized than the Red Army. Study the enemy's ways, starting with this ceremony – gruesome though it is.

I read about the circumcision ceremony in a brief encyclopedia entry and knew what to expect. I just never imagined that as a loyal officer in the SS I would have to witness such an event.

I do not deserve this.

I knocked on the Rosenbergs' door exactly at ten. The husband Jew opened the door and was quite happy to see me.

"Good morning, Johann! So glad to see you here today."

To my astonishment – and annoyance – he hugged me. I did not return his embrace but mumbled thanks and pulled away. His wife led me to a chair.

"Have a seat, Johann. I am very glad to see you on our proud occasion. Would you like something to drink?"

"A glass of water please, thank you."

If you could only imagine what I think of you ... and of all this.

"Johann is our new neighbor," explained the Jewess to the other people there. "He lives down the lane, alone. He's from Switzerland."

They all nodded towards me politely.

I am surrounded by Jews. We used to meet in different circumstances. Maybe those days will be back one day.

That thought cheered me and I began my observations of this race. They looked quite ordinary. A few wore a small piece of cloth on their head. I remembered that some of the really religious Jews did the same. I saw them in their ghettoes – and at the camps.

"We are waiting for the rabbi," the Jew husband informed me. He grabbed a chair and sat near me. "You know, today is a great occasion for our family," he said in elation.

Eager to begin my study, I asked, "What is the significance of the ceremony?"

"This is one of the most sacred ceremonies for a Jewish male. A life covenant is created between our God and the child."

His elation became earnestness.

"This is a commitment, for life, to believe in our Creator and the Torah. It's irreversible. Once you become a Jew, you can never undo it. For us, the parents, this is a great honor. I assume that you are Protestant, Johann?"

"Uh ... yes." I found my words only slowly as I had no real religion.

"It's similar to your baptism then. Were you baptized?"

"Yes, I was."

"For the Jews, it is just the beginning of the commitment. Later, when the boy reaches the age of thirteen, he goes through another ceremony – the Bar Mitzvah. There, he stands before the congregation and prays to stand by himself. From that age on, the boy is responsible for his own actions. Previously, his parents had been responsible. According to tradition, prior to the Bar Mitzvah, if the boy did wrong, the parents would be punished."

He smiled as he watched the expression of interest on my face.

"That how it was in Antiquity. Of course today, in our times ... well, it's a little different."

His eyes are so ... gentle.

"Is it too much to start with, Johann? I don't want to overload you with too much Judaic lore!"

"Oh ... perhaps a bit. Let's go more slowly with the topic."

I feigned a smile. I have to admit, it was interesting to hear of their way of life. I had developed certain curiosities during the war. Nonetheless, I was glad that he stopped the stories.

What's wrong with you? Your interest here is purely tactical. This is information about the enemy of all mankind and not anthropological analysis of an exotic tribe. Stay focused!

He patted my back in a gregarious way.

"Whenever you would like to know more about the Jewish religion, please do not be shy, Johann. We will be glad to explain anything you would like to know about it."

"Thank you. I appreciate that."

I stuck to my practiced politeness.

Filthy Jews! I don't need your Judaism. I am just studying you for the day when....

I sat, sipped from my water now and then and watched. The rabbi arrived amid much ado.

"Rabbi Levi has come all the way from Worcester," the Jew husband told me. "It's a great honor for us. His wisdom and compassion are unsurpassed! Have you ever met a rabbi before?"

I didn't reply. I couldn't reply. An old memory stabbed me. I had to force myself to focus on the rabbi's presence in the room.

He was a tall man with a long gray beard – the classic look, exactly as I saw them during the war. The old memory returned. The soldiers under my command killed a rabbi, along with his students, in a little Polish town near Lvov.

Yes, I've met a rabbi before – Rabbi Mordechai.

*   *   *

It was in a small town and we were ordered to rid it of a handful of Jews that lived there – an operation that would not even require a whole platoon. I had received my rank of first lieutenant, *Obersturmführer*, just a few weeks before and I was eager to prove my worthiness. My commander gave me this opportunity and I was determined not to fail him.

"We have a village with a small Jewish population," he told me in the briefing. "I'm sending you with twenty soldiers to cleanse the village."

He stared into me.

"You look like an ambitious young officer...."

He smiled, conveying his confidence in me, and I felt proud. *The commander likes me.*

I stood erect, like the ramrod of a fine Mauser. He looked at me once again then nodded, pleased by my response.

"Go then and make me proud. I give you one week to complete the operation."

"Ja wohl, Herr Standartenführer! I will not falter," I responded smartly.

I remember vividly the next few days. We trucked into the village before noon and easily rounded up the Jews. The locals had willingly informed us that there were only a dozen or two of them and that this time of day they could be found in their *yeshiva*, or school. We found them there in their yeshiva, reading and praying. It spared us the time-consuming task of a house-to-house search.

We took them to the marketplace to the cheers of the locals. We humiliated them by shearing their long sideburns, which had some religious significance. Some of the locals ran up to slap them and spit on them. The Jews did not even resist. How could they.

*   *   *

I opened my eyes for a moment and I was back in Webster, back in their midst. Here, I am treated nicely by Jews. They serve me water, food and treat me with respect. And I helped to kill them not too many years ago.

*   *   *

We counted about fifty students in the yeshiva. Their rabbi was a man of some character, I must say. He was a simple, decent man who tried with all his powers to convince us to leave his students alone – young men between sixteen and twenty who studied under him on a daily basis. As the officer in command, I felt compelled to listen to his reasoning, though their fate was assured.

"Sir, we do not harm anyone. We just want to study our religious texts," he said in the Yiddish dialect of our German tongue. "Please do not harm my students. I am begging you, leave them alone. They do no harm."

I was removed from my sense of duty for a moment. I sensed a good man trying to protect his people. A pious man like that could still believe that such entreaties would cause soldiers to shrink from their orders. My personal inclination would have been to leave them alone. After all, they really didn't do harm to anyone as far as I could tell. We had been told that the Jews helped partisan guerrillas that operated in the forests, but that seemed unlikely in this case. Common sense – or a basic internal sense of decency – tried to speak to me. I stood there, trying to think of a reason to kill these people. None came.

But I was an officer. The uniforms on my men and me proclaimed that, as did their rifles and machine pistols – as did the Luger in my holster.

What is wrong with you? my internal commander called out. *You are a soldier and a soldier follows his orders.*

After humiliating them in the town center for a while, we arranged them in lines and the soldiers started to shoot them. Most of the townspeople had no stomach for that, and so they returned to their homes or workplaces. None of the Jews said a word. Each simply stood there and waited his turn. Some of them whispered their prayers unintelligibly. My commands were carried through. One after the other, they fell as their rabbi stood amid them, crying quietly.

What is going through his mind? What is going through his soul?

I covered my face with my hands.

What did they do to us?

After all of his students had been shot, I approached the rabbi and saw deep sadness in his face. He was silently crying – for others. I did not know what to think. I felt I did not belong there. I felt that I wasn't there.

What nightmare is this?

A strange thought came to me. Amid the murder and madness, I felt something in me demanding to learn something. I wanted to know something about him. Who is he? What does he feel about all this? Why? I needed to bridge our two very different beings.

"What is your name?" I asked quietly.

He looked at me in surprise. He probably wondered why such a thing could matter. His expression changed. He studied my face and I got the distinct impression he saw something in me. Maybe he felt that I was different. I was the officer in charge. I was the one responsible for all this. But there was something different about me. Something ... oh, I don't know ... perhaps something *good*.

"My name is Rabbi Mordechai."

His eyes wandered into my soul. I felt ... invaded.

He knew my intent – and my resolve as well. Yet he seemed to see something.

"Do you have a last request?"

I tried to be authoritative but my voice was shaking and I had to control myself to maintain the appearance of authority in front of my men.

His eyes were filled with tears and sadness itself was on his face. His world had collapsed. He looked hopeless. But my question lit a flame inside him. I saw a glimmer of happiness, as though I had given his life back. Was I wrong?

I just told him of his impending death – and this brings gladness? Folklore has long held that Jews have magical powers. Is that what is happening?

I was trained well and fought off any sign of doubt or weakness.

As he stood there among the corpses of his students, he spoke.

"A last request, please."

I nodded.

"According to our religion, someone has to say a prayer for the dead. It is said for a mother or father – any relative or friend. Now, I'd like to say this prayer for my students."

I could not talk. Something in his voice, his look and his presence caused me to remain silent and to simply listen. We were beyond the mundane just then, and into a sacred sphere.

Some of the soldiers began joking and laughing amid the mayhem around us.

"Silence!" I barked and they complied immediately.

"What is this prayer?"

He did not expect interest from me.

"This prayer – the Kaddish – honors our God. It's a mourning ritual. It is our way to accompany the souls that are separated from us in this world. It is praise for our God for giving us life, which we now return to him."

He looked into me.

"Tradition calls for the presence of at least ten men to say the Kaddish. A *minyan*."

I looked at his dead students then back into his eyes. He did not have his *minyan*. Horror inexplicably pervaded my soul. I couldn't move. He saw my paralysis, and to my astonishment he smiled reassuringly as though to say that he understood, that it wasn't my fault. Tragic circumstances that day.

"A special case," he said as he looked at the dead bodies around him, "Today must be an exception."

His gentle look sent guilt through my soul, though I know this was not his intent.

"I will say the prayer, alone, for all of my students."

"Yes," I murmured. "Today is a special case...."

My inability to understand or to grasp what was happening must have been visible on my face. My soldiers heard him and froze. He looked at me almost as he would a good friend. He was silently encouraging me to permit the prayer.

"Say your prayers for your ... for them," I answered in a low voice.

"Please ... wait until I have finished ... I thank you for this."

Wait until he is done with the prayer before ... killing him.

"Who is going to say the prayer for you?" I asked as we stood in this sacred moment, above the earthly moments of war and bureaucracy.

He didn't answer. A notion of respect for this man was beginning to form in my mind and I had to fight it.

He doesn't think about himself, only his fellow students. Such courage and strength.... Even if we kill him, he will have won.

He neared the bodies of his students, wrapped his striped cloth atop his head and looked at me as though to say, "Please wait for my sign."

The soldiers looked at me for direction as the strange moment was making them uneasy, so distinct was it from other such operations.

My glare told them to await my sign.

He started his prayer. It sounded strange to me. It wasn't in any European language – I had heard them all. He paused a few times, turned to each side and prayed devotedly. We looked silently at a man saying a last prayer for dead friends – just before he would join them. His body moved back and forth and his entire body trembled as though in an impassioned effort to achieve perfection. He did not open his holy book. He knew the words by heart.

Strange, exotic language....

Something happened as I looked on – something I cannot explain. A moment of panic seemed to be coming on. My discipline fought it off.

Upon completion, he kissed his holy book, breathed in deeply and looked up to the heavens as his lips continued silently – a personal prayer, I thought then.

He looked at me and nodded, almost imperceptibly.

I stood in silence – and not a little awe, I can tell you.

My soldiers brought me back to our duty. No one spoke – they were subordinates. But their expressions asked for the order to finish the task. I motioned to the sergeant to finish things. I closed my eyes then heard the staccato report of a machine pistol and the sound of the rabbi's body crumple to the ground – there among his students.

That's it. Our operation here is complete. The Jewish community has been liquidated. Judenfrei....

My soldiers chatted and laughed on the way back to the encampment. For them, it had been a routine mission and a warm meal in the mess tent was in store for them.

It was not a routine operation for me. Something had been implanted in me that day, something that I dared not explore – not for many years, not until that day in Webster. Driven by my position and training, I refused to think it through. There were other such actions. Too many to remember. Soon enough I became a field-grade officer and my superiors predicted that one day I'd reach Oberführer, if not higher. I let it all go.

*   *   *

"Would you like some wine, Johann?"

Anne smiled graciously and touched my shoulder.

"It's a tradition to celebrate during this ceremony ... and drinking wine is an agreeable part of it!"

Her husband joined her and it seemed they expected conversation from me.

"Johann, we would like to ask you a personal question," he said with obvious excitement.

Ugly Jews! If I could escape from here it would be wonderful.

But there was no escape just then. I wondered if it would be better to have died in the war.

"Of course," I heard myself saying. I managed a weak smile.

"We would like to ask you to be the godfather of Samuel."

Have these people gone mad? Is this some sort of punishment?

I took a deep breath.

They know nothing about me except my proximity to their house. Maybe that's it. These people are so naive ... no judges of character at all.

I had my research to think of.

"It would be an honor."

The rabbi approached me and I could not but see him as ominous.

"I understand you are from Switzerland ... and have no family here," he said as he extended his hand.

"Yes, that is so," I replied as I reluctantly shook his hand.

"Being Samuel's *sandak* – the Hebrew word for godfather – makes you part of the family. It will give your life a whole new meaning."

Then he added in a serious tone, "May I assume you have a Protestant background?"

I nodded.

"Your religious background makes no difference. Today you become part of this house."

"Ahh...."

I was less than honored.

I held the baby as the rabbi prepared for his little operation. Samuel smiled to me, not knowing what was in store.

I recall many Jewish babies who knew not what was in store. Thrown into mass graves then buried alive.

The baby reached out to me with his little hand.

"Look, he likes you!" the mother Jew blurted out.

He really did seem to like me. He smiled and giggled. A thought began to form inside me.

"It is time," the rabbi announced happily.

I held him tightly as Rabbi Levi began with an opening prayer. Samuel's eyes said, "I trust you. This ceremony will do no harm to me. You will protect me."

I can't protect you.

The rabbi made the incision. I was confused, upset, and could not control my thoughts. Samuel's eyes registered his pain and a cry erupted from his little lungs.

"Hush ... everything will be just fine." I instinctively comforted him, holding his hand and patting his little head.

The rabbi poked his finger into the baby's mouth. I was taken aback.

What is he doing?

"It's a little wine – he will feel better soon," the rabbi explained to me, somehow sensing my question.

Samuel stopped crying and looked at me, neither blaming me nor demanding apology. He just had an explicably serious expression that babies sometimes form. It's part of their mystery.

"Here, I'll have him now. Thanks so much, Johann."

The mother Jew took him to another room – for nursing, I thought. I was left there, alone with open arms. For a second I felt an emptiness. I had sensed his pure, sweet, innocence. And that scent – the scent of a newborn.

The mothers must have felt something a million times more powerful when their babies were taken away....

The mothers' expressions ... and their screams....

One woman told her friend, "They're just taking them someplace where they will be taken care of, where they can play. I know it in my heart." The other woman looked at her incredulously. She wanted to believe her but could not. She wept as her baby was taken away with so many others – by my soldiers.

We did not kill them in front of the mothers. It wasn't a matter of considerateness; it simply caused too much tumult. We took them to the other side of the camp where they were thrown into immense pits.

Some mothers went mad and had to be killed on the spot. Others feigned acceptance, bided their time, then attacked the soldiers with their bare hands. Maternal instincts are not always gentle, I can tell you. They were immediately shot of course – but the mothers expected it.

My heart pumped erratically, my skin became cold and my mouth became parched.

I had to end this recollection.

Samuel

I NEEDED TO GET away from Webster. I drove my Ford compact over to Cape Cod and rented a cottage in Chatham, where I could reorganize my thoughts. The Jews had confused me. They knew how to do it and they'd been doing it for centuries, I then thought.

Back at the Brit ceremony, I began to feel that our work in Poland and elsewhere had been a mistake and that our Party and august leaders had misled us. I came back to my old views in time, remembering our Führer and his bold and inspiring words.

We started the historic mission of making the Jews an extinct race – not only the Jews, any minority deemed incompatible with our Aryan race. The Final Solution, we were convinced, was the right thing, but we lost the war and the Jews became free to perpetrate their work. In the United States, Jews and other minorities were gaining strength everyday.

I had followed the Nuremberg trials. I recall looking on helplessly from my seclusion as Germany's generals and leaders were convicted and executed. And some years later, in the early sixties, the Eichmann matter. The Jews hunted him down in Argentina and took him to Israel. He had to endure a racist trial, inhuman abuse and eventually a horrible execution.

I did not want to go through the same process Eichmann did, but sometimes I was convinced they would eventually hunt me down.

I also saw how these Jews created their own land – the nation of Israel. The Arabs around them fought back yet somehow the Jews managed to defeat them. They are a lucky nation. Their luck would end one day, I was sure.

I looked forward to a day when the Nazi party would rise again, although I thought it was many years away. I hoped to live to see their extermination. Yes, there would have been no happier person than I.

I sat on the porch of my cottage and watched the calm blue ocean and breathed in the salty air that a light wind had carried in along with a fine mist. I loved this part of America. The whole interaction with the Jews had made me upset – even depressed. Despite my travails, moments on the Cape shore made life worth it.

I took a large sip of Rhenish wine and looked to the sea.

I must come here more often.

I had enough money to do anything I wanted, within reason. Better to see new places.

I should spend less time with those Jews.

I stayed on the Cape all that weekend and drove home Monday night. On Tuesday morning the Jew mother knocked on my door – with her baby.

"Good morning, Johann. How are you today?"

"Good ... thank you."

I answered quite brusquely, hoping she would sense my preference for no company just then. But my intent was not understood.

"Could you do me a favor, Johann? I must go to the store to buy something ... urgent – a feminine matter, you know...."

She gave me a modest smile – as though I understood or cared.

"Could you watch little Samuel for an hour or so ... please?"

I was aghast at her intrusiveness.

"Oh ... but ... I don't know how ... I just...."

She ignored or did not see my reluctance.

"Oh, you'll do fine. Here is his bottle and diapers. They're all in the bag. I'll be back by noon."

It would become half a day. I can't do that. I am a middle-aged man – an SS officer, not a nanny for Jewish brats.

"You are Samuel's godfather … and you might want to spend more time with him. It is, after all, tradition."

She gently tapped on the baby's hand and left us.

The baby rolled to his side, opened his big blue eyes and stared at me. We stared at each other for a while. I had to shake my head.

He made a noise – and I flinched.

No need to panic. Babies make odd noises all the time.

Why did I flinch so?

*   *   *

We searched the houses of Jews and pushed everyone out onto the street. Mothers hid their babies – in attics, cellars, and compartments in walls, but babies always made noises, especially as my men tromped across the bare wooden floors in their heavy boots. In most cases, we shot the disobedient mothers on the spot. The babies were tossed out to die somewhere. No one cared for baby Jews.

*   *   *

Samuel giggled then reached out to me.

"What do you want? What are you smiling at?"

As though he understands me.

But for little Samuel, the details of language did not matter. He continued smiling with his big bright eyes – at me.

"Ahhhh, I do not have time for this."

I went to fix myself a drink.

Samuel started to cry immediately and I turned around.

"What is it?" I was annoyed and I almost shouted at him.

As I moved back toward him, his crying stopped and a warm smile spread across his face again. He reached out to me once more.

"So you want me to pick you up and take you with me?" I asked in annoyance.

He giggled joyfully. As long as he could see me, he was happy.

"I see…. Then I have to carry you around with me."

He chuckled mirthfully.

I read that babies have good instincts about good and evil. Where were this baby's instincts?

"You are all wrong, little one. I am not your protector. No, not at all."

As I held little Samuel, he looked searchingly into my eyes. To my astonishment, I became transfixed. His deep blue eyes pierced my being and his soul looked into mine. The sweet scent of a newborn filled my nostrils. He touched my chin, then my nose and brow and hair. Every detail of his face, pink cheeks, clear eyes, soft blond hair, utterly captivated me.

Tears filled my eyes and I had to sit. Something had burst inside me and dammed up emotions surged forth. I made no effort to stop them. Little Sam saw my tears and reached to catch them.

An inquisitive gurgle seemed to ask why I was crying.

"I do not know, little fellow," I answered, happy that no one else could see me. "I just do not know."

Samuel will soon forget all this, unless some essential imprint remained. But we had shared a moment of profound human understanding.

But I had to do more. I had to talk to him – confess to him.

"When I was younger, long ago ... I helped to kill many people ... many of *your* people."

He looked into me.

"Yes, I was very ... bad ... evil. Today, if anyone discovered who I am, they would probably send me to the gallows.... But you will never know that, will you? Because you are just a little baby.... A little Jewish baby ... unaware of the past ... of the man ... who is with now .... Or do you see a new man?"

I held his little hand.

"You are beautiful, do you know that? A beautiful Jewish baby."
But he is Jewish, this is not right.
I pressed Samuel to my heart for a long time.
So heartless then....
"Well, it looks like we are friends now."
He smiled and I became his prisoner.

"Awwww ... what a touching scene!"

I heard a woman's soft voice – obviously deeply moved.

"You two fell asleep!"

Anne stood before us as Samuel slumbered in my arms.

"Oh ... yes. It seems we did."

"I'll take him now and you can go back to your nap."

Anne gently took Samuel from my arms, waved goodbye and almost noiselessly closed the door. I sat alone in my living room, my arms still warm from my little friend.

Horrific images appeared in front of me with vivid cruelty. I felt cold. My mouth became dry. My heart pounded. I tried to banish the images from my head, but without success.

I need water.

I drew from the faucet, opened the blinds and looked outside. It was early afternoon and the sun sent bright beams onto the tall, green trees of rural Massachusetts. I sat there for a while until I calmed down. The sunbeams touched my face, soothing me.

I discovered that afternoon that after years of solitude and of avoiding my deepest memories, I needed to think things through and reconcile old beliefs with recent experience. I needed to be with someone. I needed to talk with someone. I needed someone to hold me. I needed someone to be with me in hard moments.

I ruefully noted that my only friend was a young child.

Sleep came and went, interrupted by evil images. Though still tired, I was glad when the first fingers of dawn appeared. I was even gladder when Anne came by with Sam.

I expressed my wish to spend more time with him, as befitting tradition, as befitting a *sandak*.

Just let me be with my friend again ... my only friend in this world.

"Oh, little Samuel. If we could just turn back the pages of history.... I would do many things differently."

I kissed his forehead.

As his hands explored my head, those memories attacked again. Shooting little babies in their mothers' arms, hurling them into mass graves, smashing their heads onto walls. I could not handle this.

"I am sorry, Samuel," I told him through my tears. "I am truly sorry for what I did to your brothers and sisters."

Samuel looked at me and gently wiped the tears from my cheeks. Maybe he was just playing but I don't think so. He continued wiping my tears and patting my hair, soothing me.

His presence – or merely thinking of him when I was alone – helped me in difficult moments.

He looked grumpy now.

Does he....

"I am sorry, little boy, you must be hungry. Please forgive old Johann for his difficult moment. Here, I'll make you a heaping bowl of rice right away."

Rice was a house specialty.

Indeed, he was hungry. After a full bowl of rice, he fell asleep in my arms. It had become a pleasant day after all.

"I would like to ask another favor, please," Anne asked that evening. "Tomorrow we are conducting a memorial service for Elliot's father, at our synagogue. Samuel will get bored and maybe even a little restless. Could you come along with us and watch Samuel, please? He behaves with you – and your presence would be an honor also. Elliot will say his prayers for his father. He will say the Kaddish prayer – our prayer of mourning. Are you familiar with it?"

I know the meaning of the prayer. I once heard a rabbi....

I fell to the floor.

I couldn't see anything. I could hear crying and someone calling my name.

Dim lights and faces....

My head ached and I felt nauseous. Samuel was sitting on the floor, crying loudly, as Anne applied a moist towel to my noggin.

"Johann, are you alright?"

"I am ... good, thank you. I just...." I mumbled as I closed my eyes and struggled against the nausea. "What happened?"

"It seems you passed out and banged your head on the chair on the way down."

"Sorry to cause you this trouble. I was a little lightheaded and must have stood up too quickly."

If she only knew....

"Come to our house. We can take care of you there."

Her worries would not pass quickly.

"No, no ... many thanks though."

I summoned a smile.

"I'll be fine. I just need some good sleep. Tomorrow, I'll be a new man."

"I'll check with you this evening – just in case. Keep your phone line open."

"Sure."

As though I routinely hear from old friends.

"I'll come by in the morning and see if you are up to attending the service."

"I'll be there," I inexplicably blurted out.

"Are you sure?"

The clarity and certainty in my voice surprised her.

"Yes, I am sure," I replied determinedly. "I think I should attend the Kaddish service. I feel ... well, obliged."

The next morning, I stood in front of a stately building in Worcester, about thirty miles north of Webster. It was a venerable synagogue with Roman and Byzantine influences dating back well into the nineteenth century.

I didn't think the Puritans in those days allowed non-Christians to build their places of worship.

Two large wooden doors graced the front, each engraved with letters I could not understand.

They could never understand me.

I arrived earlier than the family – I'm not sure why. The anticipation, maybe the fear. Or the notion that standing there before the large Star of David chiseled above the entrance might hold something for me. How many times I had seen this symbol while in the SS, I could not recall. Nor could I tell how many times I gave the command to burn synagogues. Standard procedure in those days.

Now I was about to enter a synagogue and sit inside it, holding a Jewish baby whom I was starting to love more than my own life. I would participate in a ceremony that I learned about long ago in incomprehensible circumstances.

That is why I am here today. That is why I wanted to be in this ceremony and listen to this prayer.

The last person I saw praying this prayer ... we killed him. I closed my eyes for a moment and the face of Rabbi Mordechai appeared in my mind. His long, curly sideburns, his dignity in the face of death.

*   *   *

He smiled – as though thanking me for granting his request. His eyes conveyed his thoughts more ably than any words could have.

"You are a good man – I can tell."

I froze, unable to comprehend this. I could not grasp his meaning.

"One day this war will be over ... and all this will be over.... Think...."

He has lost his mind.

"I can see inside your heart. This is not your will.... This is not determined by us ... our Lord. For everything there is a reason ... even for this."

His words tore inside me.

This is truly a holy man ... I do not want him to die.

"Humans see with their eyes. The Lord sees inside us. We see the outside only and cannot see inside."

He finished his prayer but I did not even notice. I was captivated by the sacred moment.

"Herr Standartenführer...."

One of my soldiers sought orders amid the surreal interlude.

Rabbi Mordechai saw my paralysis. Many soldiers experience this. Some are relieved of their duty and sent for psychiatric evaluation. Some were executed for cowardice.

"I've finished my prayer."

He is ready ... I am not.

Rabbi Mordechai nodded in assent and calmly wrapped himself with the striped cloth.

"Herr Standartenführer...."

I was the commander and had to give the order, but I couldn't. A private, probably nineteen years old, held his machine pistol, eager to kill another Jew.

Why does this boy yearn to kill this man?

"Herr Standartenführer!"

The young soldier's voice was almost insistent now.

I had to proceed. The rabbi's face still conveyed assent. I wanted to embed his image in my memory. There was meaning there that I could not explore then – that I *would* not explore for decades.

I motioned with my hand – more a gesture of reluctant dismissal than anything else.

The soldier aimed his machine pistol and fired. A flock of blackbirds shrieked and fled to the heavens as a dozen rounds ripped into Rabbi Mordechai and he fell under the thunderous gunfire. The soldier continued firing even after his body had reached the ground. The body seemed to convulse as the remaining bullets in the magazine hit home. The gunfire echoed off the walls and hills long after the weapon was empty.

I looked on in silence for what seemed several minutes.

Then I felt anger. My head was about to explode. I stormed over to the young soldier and hit him across the face with my Luger. I hit him with all my strength. He fell to the ground with a sharp cry. I continued kicking him until my sergeant pulled me back.

"Herr Standartenführer, what did he do?" he demanded as he breathed heavily.

I looked at the soldier lying on the ground, groaning in pain, his

'Jacob, come help us. We have to bury them.'

Bury what? It made no sense – no one buries rags. As my father looked more closely, he started to shake. The wagon was not hauling bloodstained clothing, but piles of bullet-riddled bodies.

My father wanted to run home to see about his family. But how could he refuse this request? He joined the other Jews behind the wagon, on their way to bury the dead. Overloaded with the corpses, the wagon creaked and the horses struggled.

'Let's push,' insisted the driver. Grabbing the wooden railing, my father, to his horror, saw the face of a classmate. 'Oh my God! It's Isaac!'

Isaac Cohen, or Itzeek as they used to call him, was a stocky, good-natured boy. He and my father shared the same bench at school, played together and experienced life as good friends do. Only yesterday they had played together. Now he lay dead, his head protruding grotesquely through the side railings. My father wept openly as they continued on their grim journey.

When the group arrived at their destination, they beheld a hideous scene. Countless bodies lay in a pool of blood at the bottom of a huge pit, where the machine guns had done their work. Having performed their duty for the day, the Germans had gone, leaving the area to the Polish militia, who told them to gather the corpses of those who had been shot trying to escape and to toss them into the mass grave.

After they finished their ghastly tasks, Leon the shoemaker solemnly said, 'Fellow Jews, let us say Kaddish over the grave of our brothers here.'

They lined up at the edge of the pit and began to recite the age-old prayer: *Yisgaddal veyiskadash Shmey Raba…. And the name of the Lord be sanctified and extolled.*

Standing before this mass grave of innocents and praising God seemed sacrilegious, blasphemous! My father couldn't do it. He looked around at the mourners – these broken people who with rhythmic motions repeated the sacred prayer, as their forefathers had for thousands of years. In them – in their faces and in their voices – he saw the indestructible soul of the Jewish people … the source of our strength and our weakness.

After the Kaddish, the group walked slowly and silently back towards the ghetto. Some passersby glanced at them in shock, but there were others who laughed.

As they approached the ghetto, my father's heart pounded wildly. He leaped over the border stream and ran to his house. No one was in the kitchen. A pot of blackened potatoes soaking in water sat mutely on the table. His poor mother would never leave food like that.

His whole family, he concluded, had been killed by the Nazis.

A feeling of shame stayed with my father throughout his life. He came to understand the precariousness and limitations of human existence. A man can't control his feelings and, in time of danger, he can only rarely control his deeds. Not many months ago, my father recited a Kaddish for his family, murdered in the Holocaust."

Elliot became silent, as did the congregation. Not a murmur or a breath could be heard.

"I will say Kaddish for my father now."

I wanted to stand and ask Elliot to say a Kaddish for Rabbi Mordechai – for the gentle holy man who fell among his students that day so long ago. I wanted the prayer said for him.

I do not know how to say it ... I have no right to say it.

Elliot said a Kaddish for his father that day. The entire congregation joined him.

A Second Chance

I T WAS THE OUTSET of the seventies and Samuel had become an adorable toddler. He had pure white skin and curly blond hair. His big blue eyes caught the immediate attention of all who met him. We continued to spend most days together. The Rosenbergs went to work and I tended to their son – free of charge but greatly enriched. We agreed that I'd take care of him until kindergarten.

Smart too. I was the one who helped him with his speech and vocabulary. On our walks, I'd point to various things – birds, plants and the like – and teach him their names and meaning. Samuel learned new things with breathtaking speed and that too brought comment from people. I received occasional praise as his mentor – for which I was quite proud.

As he grew up, however, I had to be more careful with our conversations. An incautious word here or there could alarm his parents and lead to who knows what.

I never loved anyone else as much I loved him. He was the only one to whom I talked freely about what bothered me. He called me by my first name. His parents tried to make him call me "Uncle Johann," but he refused. "Johann is my friend. I'll call him Johann," he insisted.

He was almost four years old and next year he would start at the Jewish kindergarten in Worcester. I did not look forward to that, although Anne wanted me to pick him up and watch him until she arrived in the evening. It would cut our time together significantly and the thought of not being with him caused me distress. But we had at

60

least six more months until then and we enjoyed our time together every day.

One cheery March day we went for a post-breakfast walk down a winding, traffic-free lane graced with beautiful trees, rustic homes and small farms. Samuel's favorite place was a farm only a short walk from my house where a half dozen horses grazed quietly. Every time we passed by, Samuel wanted to feed an especially gently and inquisitive mare.

"I brought an apple for our horse friend...."

Sam knew how to ask leading questions.

"She'll be glad to see you," I answered with a smile as I enjoyed the brisk air. He stepped up his pace and was soon a few yards ahead of me. I cautioned him, as I do every morning.

"Be careful ... watch for cars."

He nodded and continued ahead.

"Johann, do you love animals?"

"Yes, Samuel. I love animals very much."

"What about horses? Do you love horses?"

"Oh yes, I love them very much. When I was about your age my father taught me how to ride a horse. Later, I even participated in races and dressage competitions."

"What was your horse's name?"

"Bruno – a beautiful brown Arabian. I was quite fond of him ... and he of me, I can tell you."

Samuel ran to the fence enclosing the gentle horses.

"Look Johann, she's way over near the barn."

"Let's wait a bit and maybe she'll come closer," I suggested as we stood just outside the wooden fence.

We both watched the graceful horse grazing on the sparse spring grass and a bale of hay as well.

A man approached the horse carrying a stick. He was clearly agitated and to our dismay he began to beat the horse. She neighed and shrieked in pain and tried to get away. Only then did we notice she was secured to a pole.

We were aghast. And Samuel's first sight of violence caused him to cry.

"Hey, what are you doing?" I shouted at the man. "Stop hitting that poor animal!"

The man turned towards us and strode determinedly towards us.

"Stay off my property!!!" he yelled as he stormed towards us.

"We are not on your property, you fool," I yelled back. "Stop hitting that poor horse or I'll call the police."

I was genuinely angry, and even after many years I could still summon the air of authority of an officer. Had Samuel not been present, the harsher English words I had occasion to learn would have come forth readily.

The man now stood before us, shouting angrily and flailing his hands about.

"Trespassers! Go away before I shoot you!"

"We are standing on the road, which is town property."

I spoke sternly.

"Your foolish behavior and threats will land you in jail. I have a small child here. Would you harm a child?"

"Stop hitting that horse," Sam said with the look of a scolding teacher.

The man looked at him then at me.

"See, even a child recognizes senseless cruelty when he sees it. I repeat: stop hitting this animal or we'll report you to the police."

"I'll do to my animal what I want to do. It's mine and no one can tell me shit," he roared, revealing rows of blackened and rotten teeth, probably from chewing tobacco.

"You are as hideous as your nature. I would not suggest participating in any Smile of the County competitions."

I continued taunting him in a calm voice, though my accent increased with my anger. I wanted him to strike out against me so that I could punch him right back.

I can take him, even at my age.

"Hey ... you sound like a goddam foreigner!"

"And you're probably a Jew!" came my immediate though unwise riposte.

Too late. My heart raced. Did I reveal myself?

My words, though offensive, were probably part of this man's daily routine and caused no suspicion to fall on me. If anything, my outburst put fear in him.

"Go away," he muttered as he turned back to the barn.

He took the mare into the barn then stormed back to his cottage.

"You saved the horse, Johann," Samuel exclaimed proudly.

"I hope so…. Let's go back home. That's enough excitement for one day."

Back in the quiet of home, Samuel and I moved back and forth on the rocking chair, taking in the pleasant view. A flock of turkeys had come by and were poking about for seeds near the fence in the front.

"You were very brave today, Johann," said Samuel in time. "You saved the horse from that bad man."

He softly added something he had probably heard from his parents quite often.

"Johann, I am proud of you."

"Thank you, Samuel…. It's not nice to see cruelty. When we see someone being cruel, we should try to help."

Samuel thought about this.

"Did you ever see people being cruel to other people?"

My emotional response by now must be obvious. It had been some time since those images had stabbed me. I thought their power was gone…. I took a deep breath.

"Yes, Samuel. I have seen horrible things."

I looked straight into his blue eyes.

"What did you see, Johann?"

I shook my head and patted his head.

"You do not want to know, Samuel."

Tears crept into my eyes and I tried to hide them. How could I tell him what I saw and what I did?

"Are you crying, Johann?"

An observant lad. I could not lie to him. I never did.

"Yes ... yes, I am crying."

"Why?"

His eyes searched for understanding.

"Just because...."

"Because of what, Johann? You can tell me ... I'm your friend."

I love his innocence.

"I'll never tell anyone," he added with an earnest look, as though determined to keep a secret.

"Well, Samuel, how can I put it.... Bad things ... terrible things."

I searched for words – words that a four-year-old could grasp, words that a four-year-old could comprehend without damaging his soul. I looked thought the window at the clear blue skies.

Under these same skies I committed horrible crimes.

"You were mean to horses?"

"No," I replied with a weak smile. "I was not nice to people ... many years ago."

"But why, Johann?" he asked after a moment of pondering how his hero, his best friend, the man who just saved the horse, had not been nice to people.

"I don't know, Samuel."

I was not being evasive or stalling for time until an answer came to me. I thought I knew then – all notions of the Aryan supremacy, the Party's vision, the evil of Jewry. But they weren't satisfactory. I repeated my words aloud to Samuel, and though I could not feel pleased, at least I had told him the truth. I simply did not know.

We were both silent for quite a while. Samuel was reasoning things out. It was a lot for a boy his age to handle.

Have I just lost my best friend, my only friend in this world? If I have, I'll understand. I would not want anything to do with a person like me. Maybe Plan O was not good. Living like this ... better to have died.

"You are good now.... You are a good man now, Johann.... You just saved the horse from the bad man."

Tears flowed, but I found more than solace in his reasoning. I saw recognition of change in me.

"Yes, I did ... I did at that, didn't I."

"And you are my best friend...."

"Yes, I am indeed," I acknowledged with a faint but strengthening smile.

"And we are together every day...."

His eyes sparkled.

He really loves me. I love him.

"Yes!"

I pressed him to my heart.

"And we will be friends forever," he concluded joyfully.

"Yes!"

I kissed him on his precious forehead.

He means everything to me.

"See! You *are* good man. Whatever made you do bad ... it's gone."

"Samuel, now I have a question for you."

I sat in front of him as my eyes dried.

"Do you think I can have a second chance?"

"What's a second chance?"

"Well, a second chance is when a person does good things after ... after he did bad things. A second chance is trying to fix the bad things that were done many years ago. Fixing bad things with good things now ... so that we can live with ourselves and go on with our lives."

I looked at him, awaiting his verdict.

"Yes, you can have a second chance. You are already good now.... We can go on."

His simple logic provided the answer.

"Thanks...."

I sank into my thoughts, enjoying them more than I had in a long time.

A little boy has given me a second chance.

Judaism

"WILL YOU COME WITH us to our Rosh Hashanah service, Johann?" Anne asked one morning. "It's our New Year."

"Oh...."

I searched for an excuse. The service for Elliot's father had caused considerable dismay. But I thought a moment....

"Yes, I'd love to come with you."

"Great!" Anne's face lit up. "I know a little boy who will be ecstatic."

"Of course, Anne. I'm his *sandak*."

"Ah, you two have a special bond. He'll always remember you – always. You are one of the most important people in his life."

"My pleasure."

Anne and I had grown closer recently. Gone were the mute resentments of my influence upon Sam. We shared thoughts on Samuel's growth and behavior, his hopes and habits. I sometimes found myself wanting to tell her of my past, but I could not. That would risk too much. My time with Sam was important to me. It was, I felt, taking me someplace.

"We are set then, next Monday at five pm at the Worcester synagogue. We'll all be there. Let me know if you need a lift."

"Thanks, I'll get there fine – I'm not that old!"

Upon reflection I looked forward to being in the synagogue again. Despite the unpleasantness of my previous visit, I experienced a soothing feeling and a strange sense of belonging, at least after a while. I had never found anything like that in church back in Germany, nor in any church in America during any of my infrequent visits.

I was the first to arrive. Again, I stood in front of the majestic old synagogue and looked up at the Hebrew motifs that decorated the archways above the entrances. I shook my head and banished the evil memories to a dark, semi-forgotten corner of my mind where I rarely ventured.

Their synagogue has stood for well over a hundred years. How long did our Reich last?

As the congregation started to arrive they greeted me warmly. I did the same, as best I could. I entered the synagogue, sat towards a back corner and looked about, appreciating artwork and intricacies that I hadn't before noted. In front stood the Bible's main cabinet, beautifully appointed with all kinds of letters and images engraved in the dark mahogany wood.

A magnificent artist must have done this. His way of giving glory....

Pictures that dealt with epic events and great prophets adorned the walls. Yes, I recognized Moses leading his people – an image I knew from distant Sunday school instruction. Those classes left little mark on me.

Anne, Elliot and little Samuel were sitting well in front of me. The little one made his seating preference known to all.

"Johann, come sit with us!"

"Alright. I'll join you if you insist."

Samuel jumped on my lap without warning just as the congregation hushed and the rabbi began.

"Thank you for coming to our Rosh Hashanah service this evening."

As everyone became focused on the rites and prayers, which were largely incomprehensible to me, I retreated into my thoughts.

The beauty of the chamber gave me the freedom to enjoy a stream of consciousness. I closed my eyes.

I liked this Rabbi Levi. His words and gestures conveyed an involvement and concern with others in the room. He was a tall, slender man, about fifty, with a long beard and an engaging spirit.

Ah, clear blue eyes as well. Well, here's a good one for the purveyors of the Aryan race myths. They saw such eyes as distinctive traits of the Teutonic peoples and highly prized them in the SS breeding programs.

Rabbi Levi was always so pleasant, ever offering help to everyone. He at times tried to engage me in conversation, but I politely declined. He sensed something wrong though he could not figure out what it was. It seemed he was patiently waiting for a chance to talk with me and to help me.

He talked about the new year and the upcoming Yom Kippur – the Day of Atonement. These times were for looking into the soul, finding bad things that we did in the previous year and asking forgiveness. Asking forgiveness from God, asking forgiveness from other people whom we offended – even unintentionally.

I cannot ask for forgiveness. Not for what I have done. My sins are far beyond the power of a simple rite.

I realized, more fully than before, at a deeper level in my being, that the Jews are not sub-humans, thieves, liars and monsters. They were human beings who believed in their God and values. They believed in the Ten Commandments. They believed in helping each other, regardless of religion. I closed my eyes as I felt pain throughout my body.

"Now is the time to think about forgiveness."

The rabbi's words reverberated as he paused.

"During the next few weeks we must cleanse our souls and prepare for the New Year, in personal resolution."

"Not for me," I murmured.

"It is for *everyone*!"

His voice sounds so....

While my eyes were closed, he had walked into the congregation and was now standing close to me. He gave me a pointed look.

He must have heard me.

"The purification process is for *everyone*. It does not matter what you have done in the past."

Each word was enunciated slowly and powerfully.

I'm sure he heard me.

"Forgiveness is for all ... it is for *you*!"

I could not look at him again during the service. I returned to my thoughts as I looked about at the congregants. Afterwards the rabbi approached me.

"Hello Johann – and how are you this fine day?"

He smiled and shook my hand.

"Quite well, thank you."

I took hold of Samuel's hand as an excuse to get away.

"It appears my little friend is a bit restless. I apologize."

He recognized my rebuff.

"Of course, if you want to talk anytime, just let me know."

"Thank you," I responded curtly.

"About *anything*," he added.

He really wants to talk with me. He wants to know what I'm hiding.

"Of course, and thank you. Come Samuel, we have to be on."

A few days later I found myself standing in front of the synagogue, alone. It was late evening and only a few people were coming out, on their way to their homes and families. I entered the now dimly lit chamber and sat in my back corner. I could not see Rabbi Levi. I felt relief, as though I had been able to avoid an unwelcome task.

Maybe I'll not have to meet him after all.

Another part of me felt disappointment, though I did not know just why.

I sat alone.

"Good evening, Johann."

His voice startled me. It seemed to boom as it resonated with the acoustics of the chamber. My nervousness added to his voice's impact on me.

"Good evening, Rabbi Levi."

Silence.

"So, what should we talk about then, Johann?"

When I did not answer, he searched for engagement.

"I know you are not Jewish.... Have you ever spoken with a rabbi before?"

"Well.... No, not really ... not like this."

He sat near me.

"What bothers you, Johann?"

I took a deep breath.

"Nothing in particular."

My answer did not sound convincing, I'm sure.

He smiled.

"Well, you are here, aren't you? That suggests you have questions ... or something that you want to talk about.... I am here."

I remained silent and sat there uncomfortably. The tension became almost unbearable to me.

I wanted to speak out, to tell him everything. I wanted to tell him about having been an SS officer. I wanted to tell him about the Jews I'd helped kill. I wanted to tell him about the horrific things we did then – and that the second chance Samuel had granted me was simply not enough.

I wanted to tell him but I could not ... and the impulse soon floated away into the void of the room.

"Why did you say you cannot be forgiven?"

He did hear me.

"Because it's true," I replied almost instantly.

Rabbi Levi paused. His forehead wrinkled in curiosity, though perhaps more with concern.

"Why is that, Johann? You look like a good person.... I've heard many bad things in my life – you can tell me.... Everything that you tell me here this night will remain between us, I promise you."

I looked at him carefully. I liked him and could see that the man had a good soul. My entire being wanted to tell him who I was, what

I'd done and the guilt that I have to carry with me until the end of my life. One day, I will have to stand trial in front of someone greater than man.

The rabbi saw my inner turmoil and sought to alleviate it.

"Humans see with their eyes, God sees into the heart. That means that we people see only external things. We see with our eyes, but God sees inside our hearts."

He let the meaning sink in.

"So you see, God sees inside of you. He knows, I'm sure, that you are a good man."

I looked at him and wondered.

*   *   *

A young child, maybe eight years old, was on a wood-gathering detail with his father and others near a camp I commanded. It was Treblinka I, a work camp that was part of a notorious system in Poland, nor far north of Warsaw. The father was quite weak and could barely do his work in the summer heat. There were old people working too. I watched silently from the backseat of my staff car as they toiled so as to avoid selection for transfer to a death camp.

Their faces showed utter despair. They moved about hopelessly in their work, like grotesque, emaciated marionettes. A sudden thought penetrated my mind, what the hell are we doing? These are humans – human beings guilty of nothing except being Jews. We are working them to death.

My soul quaked.

"Water … please. I need water!" the father cried out to the guard.

"No water, you filthy Jew," the guard spat back at him. "Keep working."

The man stumbled and fell and the boy ran to help him.

"Move away!" the guard shouted at the child. "I'll show you about taking breaks without my permission."

The child looked on in horror as the soldier leveled his rifle and shot the man there in front of everyone. The boy screamed out in anguish as the soldier pulled back the bolt of his rifle and fired two more shots into the poor man.

"This is what happens to those who do not listen!" the soldiers warned the others.

The boy's face displayed the collapse of his world. His eyes conveyed utter disbelief as he bent over his father's lifeless form.

I also recall that I screamed – a high-pitch scream that I did not think I was capable of and that caught the soldiers' attention. Suddenly my pistol was aimed at the guard's head as I shook with rage. I do not remember jumping out of the car and running to the scene, though I must have. The laborers were frightened, but also astonished by my behavior. A camp commandant is angry because a worker was shot?

The soldiers stood still, sharing the astonishment of the laborers. I pressed the muzzle of my Luger against his temple.

"How does it feel?" I roared into his ear. "How does it feel to know I can kill you merely because it pleases me – just as you killed that man?"

A sergeant tried to defuse the situation.

"Herr commandant...."

I crashed the butt of my Luger down upon the guard's head with all my power and he fell to the ground writhing in pain. I turned and glared at the other soldiers.

"Never again shoot a worker without my permission! Not you, not anyone! We need every worker to complete our work on time. I have deadlines to meet and I intend to meet them. Every worker is needed. No one kills without my permission!"

Word reached higher authorities shortly later and I had to face a hearing. But I knew how to handle such things. I smartly entered the courtroom and saluted crisply with my right arm extended upward. I stated confidently that my concern was only with the efficient use of human resources and of course in fulfilling my work for the Reich. They believed me. After all, I had an excellent record and the allegations of a few soldiers amid an immense war did not amount to much.

I had been happy when I was taken off of village roundups and assigned to the Treblinka work camp. From now on, I thought, I'd deal only with production for the war effort. Treblinka I provided gravel for roads stretching out to support our armies fighting the Bolsheviks. That was an agenda I felt more comfortable with and I put all my energies into it.

At first I saw the conditions at labor camps to be sufficient to keep workers in place to meet production schedules, but soon enough it was clear that they were worked to exhaustion – no, worked to death. Further, the workers were subject to the whims of sadistic guards. Some made workers run about from place to place for no reason whatsoever. Others humiliated them at the outhouses.

I was appalled when I first saw a guard shoot a worker for no reason. I demanded an explanation and fellow officers and guards alike promptly informed me that this was a privilege extended to guards and that it was essential to keep discipline among the inmates.

Nonetheless, I halted summary executions in my camp – or at least I tried to. I had production schedules and strove to keep them. I wanted to be a successful officer and contribute my part to the war. My schedules were met and often exceeded. Commendations came my way, as did a promotion or two.

Meeting schedules and receiving praise were not enough. I became depressed as I became immersed in the horrid means of prosecuting the war – a war whose wisdom and morality I occasionally allowed myself to doubt. My career went well, not so my soul....

*   *   *

Rabbi Levi sat wordlessly. He saw thoughts racing through my mind and waited for my account.

"No, there is no excuse for what I've done."

I stood up to leave.

"Wait ... Johann."

He gave me a look of deep concern.

"Whatever you did, it can't be so terrible."

"It's worse than terrible, Rabbi Levi."

My face must have looked stricken as I left.

First Prayer

ONE MORNING, ANNE DID not bring my friend. When I called she said he had a virus and she'd stay home with him for the next day or two. I missed him terribly. On the second day I went to visit. Samuel looked pretty well. He was happy to see me and wanted to sit on my lap – good signs, I thought.

"It should pass within another day or so," Anne told me as she brought me tea. "That's what the doctor said."

It barely registered with me as I doted on Sam.

"How's the little boy?" I asked on the third morning.

Anne's voice was tired and worried.

"He had a high fever last night so Elliot took him to the emergency room at Memorial Hospital over in Worcester, and he was admitted."

"Hospital?" I repeated in astonishment. "But Samuel's a very healthy boy – only an occasional cold."

I did not want to believe that he might be seriously ill.

"Well, it's more than just a virus," she continued. "The doctors think it may be meningitis."

I was not familiar with that sickness.

"What is it? Is it bad?"

I wanted answers.

"It's an infection of the brain. They're running some tests to confirm the diagnosis."

I didn't know what to say.

"If it is meningitis, it's very bad, Johann."

Anne's voice cracked and she sobbed.

"He will be on a series of antibiotics for several weeks. Then … we'll know more."

"A few weeks in hospital…." I mumbled in disbelief. "I'm going to see him."

Samuel lay there on a large bed, his face almost as white as the hospital bed sheets. His eyes were closed.

"He's been sleeping for the past hour," Elliot told me as he motioned me to be silent. "Here, you can have my chair."

I did not want to sit.

"How is he doing?" I whispered.

Elliot shook his head and his eyes teared up.

"Not well. The doctors are unsure of the diagnosis. They're running tests and trying various antibiotics. Nothing's helped so far…. I did not want to tell this to Anne, but the doctors are unsure if he'll pull through."

"What?"

My world teetered near collapse.

"How can it be? He's young and healthy. It can't be anything we can't beat."

It was all too much to comprehend. I had to sit now.

"I'm sure they will find the right medications and he'll be just fine," I told Elliot with all the conviction in me.

I sat near Sam and took his little hand in mine. It was pink and warm.

"See," I told Elliot confidently, "his hands feel quite healthy – he'll be just fine. All kids are like that. They get sick and just like that, they're back playing outside with their friends."

"I hope so, Johann … I hope so," he replied in a low voice to hide his emotion.

Anne arrived to stay the night and Elliot headed home. I sat near Sam's bed, determined to wait for him to wake up. My confidence came and went as the hours passed. A doctor arrived and talked with Anne in the hall. She returned distraught. There were dark circles under her eyes.

"They're continuing with all sorts of things, but they still don't know just what he has."

"Can they bring in specialists? Maybe from out of state? Overseas?"

My desperation must have shown.

"We're trying to contact a pediatric neurologist in Chicago. He can be here next week."

"Why next week? We need him now! I'll pay for his flight and fees. That's no issue here."

"You're shaking. When was the last time you ate or drank something, Johann?"

I was too weak to answer.

"Johann, listen to me. You have to eat and drink something. We all have to be strong now. We have to be strong for Samuel. We are his strength. Do you understand?"

"Yes, but when was the last time *you* rested or ate something?"

Her eyes went downwards.

"I'll get something from the cafeteria ... for both of us."

So small a lad on such a large bed, so innocent and pure. He cannot die. It would just not be right. A person like me lives and he dies? That should not be.

My soul rose against the injustice.

"Samuel . . ." I whispered, "you cannot leave us. You are too young ... and too good. You have to beat this."

I looked through the window and saw a large moon. It was a clear night and the stars in their thousands sparkled obliviously to the affairs below.

"There is one who deserves to die in this room – and it is not you. You are a pure, good soul. You've never harmed anyone ... ever. You need to live, Samuel – for your parents, for the world ... and for me."

I drowsed for a few minutes. I couldn't help it. Awake or asleep, my thoughts remained on the health of my little friend.

Did he just move?

I watched intently.

Yes, he slowly moved his head ... towards me!

And he opened his eyes!

He squinted as even the dim lighting in the hospital room seemed bright. I could not speak or move. Then he smiled weakly, squeezed my hand gently and murmured my name.

"Johann ... Johann ... why you are crying?"

"I am not crying anymore, Samuel. How do you feel?" I asked, finding new strength.

My hope was cautious. I knew that people came in and out of comas.

"I am good," he whispered.

He still looked quite ill.

"Well then, so am I."

Neither of us knew any words to use at that moment, but we knew how each of us felt.

"Would you like to eat something, my little friend?"

"Not now.... What will happen to me, Johann?"

The question caught me off guard.

"You will get better and go back home," I replied with an encouraging smile.

Samuel's look expressed that he was not sure that was going to happen.

"Why are mom and dad so sad?"

"That is because they want you back home. They do not want you here. No parents like it when their precious child is away from home. They love their children with all their hearts."

He looked to the window, no longer interested in my words.

"I'm tired...."

He closed his eyes and drifted back into sleep.

"Then rest, Samuel, just rest."

Every half hour or so, a black nurse came in. She jotted down some readings and left. I held Sam's hand and waited – for what, I do not know. A sign? Good news from a doctor? A miracle? All of them. I just wanted to be back home with him the way it had been for so many years.

Fight.... Fight, Samuel. Don't let it win.

*   *   *

An old bearded man, wrapped with the striped cloth – a *tallit* – knelt down in the snow and shook his fist at my men and me as we did our work in another village. The Jews had been rousted from their quarter and brought to the marketplace. They were for the most part unremarkable, but there was one old Jew who was in the middle of his prayer. The soldiers were already shooting people here and there, and enjoying their work and the horrified screams it brought. That one man wrapped himself with the *tallit*, fell on his knees then shook his fist and looked to the skies.

"Another crazy Jew," a couple of soldiers joked.

They would mock them and kill them, but my previous behavior made them recognize that certain individual Jews, especially pious ones, had a strange impact on me. I watched this old Jew – a rabbi, I believe.

Fight! Fight for your life! Why don't you fight?

I wanted him to do the improbable. I wanted him to fight back – to kill a soldier or two before they killed him. Maybe it was my military upbringing, but I could not understand not fighting back. The rabbi just shook his fist at us and prayed.

My soldiers looked at me, awaiting my instructions. Again, I hesitated. Then I turned around and walked back towards my staff car. My sergeant ran after me, asking what to do. I walked away as fast as I could but he closed and asked, "What should I do with him, Herr Standartenführer?"

I fell into another a rage.

"What do you mean what to do with him? What kind of idiot are you? What do you do with the rest of the Jews?"

"Herr Standartenführer, I will do it immediately."

He saluted crisply and returned to his work. I did not look, I only stared above and awaited the familiar sound. The sharp, conclusive sound arrived shortly.

A Mauser this time.

I closed the car door and sat for a while – drained. I felt angry that I could not prevent this. My anger was directed squarely on me now.

"Go!" I yelled to my driver. "Go anywhere! Away from here!"

We drove from the slaughter and into the surrounding countryside. The pastoral scenery calmed me. I opened the rear window and allowed the wintery air to hit my face. I closed my eyes and enjoyed the feeling of escape from all the hideousness, short-lived though I knew it would be. There would be other villages. There would be other rabbis.

*   *   *

A soft voice stirred me.

"Johann.... Johann...."

Anne's hand lay on my shoulder and I panicked in the liminal world between sleep and consciousness.

Did she see those dreadful images? Did I speak of that day? Does she know about me now?

Then I realized I had been asleep. I could only hope that I had been silent.

"Oh ... Anne...."

"Thank you for being here. Would you like coffee and a sandwich from downstairs?"

"Please ... thank you."

I sipped the weak cafeteria coffee as Anne spoke with the doctor, who was about to leave for the night.

"Well?"

"The lab tests were inconclusive. We'll have to wait for the specialist from Chicago."

"Sam stirred ... only briefly. We spoke a bit. He sounded good. He'll be fine," I said encouragingly.

"With God's help ... with God's help."

She spoke with unconditional faith, and for that I admired her. The meaning of her words slowly sunk in.

"Yes," I found myself repeating, "with God's help."

The next weeks were pure torment for all of us. Samuel was only rarely awake and usually took in nourishment only through a tube. The neurologist from Chicago arrived but was unable to identify the disease either. He was sure the illness was new to the annals of medicine.

He could only promise us that he'd disseminate information on Samuel's illness to experts around the world and await their responses. The collective learning of scores of neurologist would be looking into Sam's affliction. The doctor returned to Chicago the next day, frustrated.

The Rosenbergs could hardly work or function. As for me, I lived in denial. Many days I had assumed that it was just a matter of time until Samuel came through. I could not comprehend the possibility of his not recovering; I could not handle that prospect. I came every day to the hospital, sometimes with Elliot or Anne, but often on my own. I spoke to him, fed him when he was awake, and took him on short excursions down the hallway in a wheelchair. I all but moved into the hospital.

I arrived one morning to find Anne and Elliot in the reception area, alone, looking despondent. The scene betokened crisis.

"What's happened?" I demanded as fear spread within me.

"He fell into a deep coma early this morning," Elliot said in a despairing voice.

Anne did not respond at all. She could not even look at me.

I rushed upstairs.

Samuel lay there motionless, though for all the world as in a sweet sleep. A slight smile formed on his lips, I thought. The idea that he may not wake up stabbed me and a profound sadness fell over me as though my purpose here in life was gone. This little child had become everything for me – a friend, a companion, but most importantly a bridge. Samuel was a bridge from my cruel, murderous past to ...

well, it had not yet formed completely by then, but to a new man who accepted humanity in all its forms.

With Samuel's simple, childlike logic I learned that life – any life – is to be cherished. And I learned that there could still be meaning in my life. I had wanted to kill, then I wanted to die. His light illuminated my darkness. His soul caressed mine and gave it hope – the hope I could do something good before my life ended, the hope to create one bright star in the dark skies, the hope to redeem myself.

I wept. Tears rolled uncontrollably down my cheeks. I could neither move nor speak. All I knew was that I was crying. I cried silently. I cried because I loved him and felt helpless. I cried because I could not help Samuel and I did not want him to die. I cried because I did not want to be left alone in this world. I cried because he was my bridge to redemption.

"Johann, you need something to eat." Anne's voice brought me back to the present. She handed me something or another.

"Thank, you Anne," I said quietly, "but I'm not hungry."

Something registered inside me and I knew what I had to do. I knew where I had to go.

I entered the synagogue and sat at my regular seat. The pleasant scent of leather and wood greeted me. I felt tranquil, as I knew I would, as I had not felt since Sam had fallen ill.

How paradoxical that I should find peace in a synagogue.

I sat there as a handful of the faithful recited their Hebrew prayers in front of me. I closed my eyes and let the prayers soothe me, though I knew not one word of them.

Holiness ... serenity ... goodness.

I could not understand the Jews who simply stood and prayed. Even amid the carnage around them, as their fellow Jews were slaughtered, they did not lose faith. They prayed. Moments from death, they immersed themselves in their rites. What were they thinking? What were they feeling? The closer they came to death, the greater their devotion.

I noticed soldiers who were struck by the sight of such piety. Some hesitated before shooting – I observed that countless times. Today, I am pleased that some hesitated. Some would allow them to finish their prayers, as did I. Such strength. Such faith.

Their prayers completed, they closed their books and looked at us, waiting – waiting to be shot. Some looked straight into our eyes. Afterwards, I occasionally heard a soldier express puzzlement – even admiration. Many of them had to be transferred to other duties.

I did not want them to be killed, but I had no choice for I was the commander – part of an immense, dreadful machine. Their faces showed calm, ours hid fear. They were shot, but we were punished. Yes, they were dead but our souls had to endure life. We went deeper into darkness, closer to hell. We deserve every bit of it.

"Hello, Johann."

"Hello, Rabbi Levi."

I felt ashamed whenever he approached me. I realized that then.

"I understand our little friend is not doing well."

His face conveyed concern and compassion.

"He slipped into a coma this morning," I replied blankly.

"I'm sorry to hear that," he replied nodding solemnly.

We both fell silent.

"Can I help in any way?"

I looked into his eyes, mine were in tears. He took my hand.

"Samuel is in the hands of a power greater than ours, Johann. We have to have faith."

"I wanted…."

My voice failed me, but Rabbi Levi encouraged me to continue.

"I wanted … to pray for Samuel. I know that you have prayers for the sick, but I do not know how to say them."

"Yes we do. I can help you say these prayers."

I cast my eyes downward. I was ashamed to make such a request in this holy place but I desperately wanted to do this for Samuel. The rabbi hugged me. I felt uncomfortable and wanted to get away … but after a moment I found myself returning his embrace.

He led me to the front.

"You may repeat after me."

I nodded.

Rabbi Levi took me to the front where an ornate wooden cabinet held a magnificent Torah book with a metal frame cover engraved with Biblical symbols and images. I had seen the faithful holding the Torah, rejoicing as it was carried about the synagogue. Many touched and kissed the Torah as it passed by, seeking to partake of its holiness.

I felt fear.

This is a holy book, the holy Bible of the Jews. My mere presence might bring down retribution on me and on those I love.

But I felt Samuel's goodness and faith and I stood there quietly.

Rabbi Levi began the ancient Jewish prayer for the sick. He spoke slowly, for my benefit, and I repeated his words as best I could.

I am standing here reciting a Jewish prayer. Who could have imagined this?

Rabbi Levi looked at me and nodded. I had a feeling that he sensed a special moment for me. I recited the words for Samuel but felt something else. With every word, I felt my soul changing – leaving something behind and heading towards something else. After we completed the short prayer we stood quietly, there by the Torah.

He stood near me, studied me, then clasped his hand on my shoulder.

"What are you feeling, Johann?"

Speechless, I raised my eyes to meet his, but I could not reply.

"You've just said your first Jewish prayer. Well ... how do you feel about it?"

How could I then express my feelings? An answer slowly formed and my eyes brightened.

"I know Samuel will get better, Rabbi Levi – I can feel it!"

He nodded.

"We all hope so, Johann. We all hope so."

He stood as though about to go, but I was not yet ready. I had more thoughts that needed to form and work through me.

"Good prevails," I whispered to myself.

"I don't...."

"Good prevails," I repeated as I exited the synagogue.

Rabbi Levi was perplexed, but he joined me and murmured, "Yes, good prevails...."

I wondered if he understood precisely what I meant.

I could not sleep well. I was haunted again by the war. I woke up in the morning still tired but went off to the hospital anyway. Anne and Elliot were there. When I stood in the doorway of the room they looked at me as though I had been the key to their son's recovery. After the weeks of sadness and hopelessness, that morning I sensed hope – maybe even elation.

"What's happened?" I asked surprised to see them so buoyant.

Then as I entered and looked towards the bed, my heart paused. Sam was sitting up in bed and eagerly eating a breakfast of cereal and raisins.

I closed my eyes unable to comprehend what I was seeing. I reopened them and felt a flood of joy. Anne and Elliot were speechless. Then the miracle boy spoke.

"Look – I'm eating breakfast!" he announced exuberantly.

I went to his bed and took him in my arms. My eyes were full of tears but it was the most beautiful day of my life. The sun shone brightly that morning and its light filled the entire world.

Ruth

IN A WAY THAT can only be called miraculous, Sam recovered within a week and life returned to normal, as surely as the seasons come back unto themselves. The doctors continued to run tests and the specialists around the globe sent in their thoughts, but no one came up with an adequate explanation for his illness – or his recovery for that matter. No known illness corresponded closely to Sam's symptoms and the values from his samples and readings.

The doctors and even the specialist from Chicago merely shrugged their shoulders and said that it was a virus that ran its course. Some viruses do it quickly, within a few days, while some take weeks. In Sam's case, the virus was a tough one. In an odd way, the doctors were frustrated that the illness vanished without a trace. A trace would have allowed further research. We were not frustrated by that. Not in the least.

Needless to say, I had my own opinion on how the virus disappeared, but I kept my non-medical, purely inexpert opinion strictly to myself. My view did not lead to advancements in medical theory, though I would never say that no benefits ever came from it.

"Good morning!" Anne gave me an especially bright smile as she led Samuel inside. "It's my first full day back to work. Here are Samuel's blanket, extra clothes and some toys of course."

He ran and leapt into my eager arms. I looked into his joyous eyes.

"Thank you, Anne. It's going to be a beautiful sunny day and I've prepared for a happy day with my friend."

"Hanukkah vacation starts tomorrow. Ten whole days together for you guys."

She was happy for me.

"Hey Johann, can we go for a walk," Samuel asked in near euphoria. "I've missed seeing all the animals and things."

"I guess my presence is not needed anymore," Anne noted somewhat glumly.

"No worries. By the time you come back he'll be ready for his mom. Now he's anxious to get out in the sun. Can you blame him?"

"Nope. Have a wonderful day, you two."

Anne kissed little Samuel and left for work.

I packed some water and snacks for the road then said, "Little boy, let's greet the sun and the animals and whatever comes our way."

We headed for a charming neighborhood called Blueberry Hill, which started at the main road and curled up to a promontory overlooking a rolling countryside. Along the lane leading up to it were quaint houses with manicured lawns and flowers that seemed to be in bloom most of the year. Only heavy snow hid the lush cover of the old pines. That day the lovely weather added a special beauty. The bracing morning air hit our nostrils and energized us.

There were no cars that day. The chirping of birds were the only sounds. This was the beauty of this area. It all made for a wondrous outing for a middle-aged man and a young boy. We could have walked for hours that day. Sam was quite well again.

I noticed that one of the houses had a Menorah in the window. I knew it was a sign of Hanukkah though the exact significance and historical basis were unknown to me.

A Jewish home.... I used to see many of those.

The front door opened and a woman in her mid-fifties came out. She was rather tall, with brown hair, and attired warmly for the day. She walked gracefully, even regally – at least to one lonely man her age. When she saw us, a smile spread across her delicate face. I was startled by her beauty.

"Good morning, gentlemen. And what brings you to our neighborhood on such a beautiful day?"

Her voice was deep yet soft – incongruous for a woman of her age. As she neared us, her beautiful green eyes looked straight at me.

"Oh, just enjoying our morning walk, madam."

I had my usual defensive formality. After a brief exchange of pleasantries, I found myself continuing.

"May I ask the lady's name, please?"

"But of course. The name is Ruth."

She emitted a charming smile and I felt things I hadn't enjoyed in years.

Ruth....

The name flowed through my mind and I thought it was the most beautiful name in the world. But where had I heard this name before? I tried to remember but could not focus at that moment.

"It's a pleasure to meet you, Ruth. My name is Johann and this little guy here is Samuel. He is almost four years old and for obvious reasons, I am obliged to tell you my age."

European manners insisted. I smiled and gently bowed.

"Oh, at our ages, you don't have to tell me anything about that subject!"

She leaned toward Samuel and greeted him with charm and grace. I detected a European accent of some sort or another.

Samuel hid behind me.

"Samuel, why are you so bashful? Please say hello to the nice lady. She's our neighbor."

Samuel peaked out from his hiding place and haltingly said, "We're ... going for a walk in here...."

"What a lovely day for a walk! And is this your grandpa?"

"He's not my grandpa, he's my best friend!"

Samuel hugged his hiding place's stout appendage.

"I am a neighbor who has had the honor and privilege of sitting for him since he was quite young," I added with obvious pride.

"Ahhh, how nice! I see that he loves you very, very much."

"Yes, he means a lot to me. He just recovered from a serious illness."

"Really? What did he have?"

"The doctors never determined that. Only last week he was in a coma."

She covered her mouth in surprise.

"But believe it or not, he came out of it – just like that."

"I'm so glad to hear that. It's hard to imagine a child having to endure such an ordeal."

Her face reflected genuine sadness.

"It was a very hard time for me as well. You see, I live alone – except for my friend's daily visits."

"I see that. You both are lucky then."

"Indeed we are … indeed we are."

Our eyes met and we remained transfixed for some time. I looked into her green eyes and … oh, I just sank into them. I was pulled in, actually.

"Let's go!"

A bit restive from the grown-up chat, Samuel tugged on my hand, which brought a little laughter from Ruth and me.

"Oh yes, we have to complete our walk."

"Of course," she smiled to us. "It was my pleasure to meet you gentlemen."

"The pleasure was all ours," I responded.

"The pleasure was all ours," said a little echo.

"Next time you come by, I'll invite you in for juice and coffee. I may also bake chocolate cookies!"

The prospect elated me.

"I live at the bottom of Blueberry Hill. If you find yourself down there, you are more than welcome to stop in."

"Thank you. I'll remember that."

We stood there, a bit awkwardly. Neither of us wanted to part. But there was another party to consider.

"Johann…."

"Yes, sure. Let's go then."

I waved goodbye as we left Ruth's yard. I looked back and saw her entering a gray Volvo. I had the distinct feeling that a change was coming into my life.

Samuel could see that I was taken by her. From that morning on, we took the same route. "You just want to see Ruth again," he teased.

"Yes, I like her. She is a very pleasant lady. I want to know more about her."

I did not hide that fact from him, nor could I had I wanted to.

"The name Ruth ... is familiar to me, but I cannot place it," I said aloud. But to a lad of his age, it meant nothing.

We started to walk every day near Ruth's house, but we never saw her. I could not figure out if she was married. I didn't recall seeing a ring though I couldn't be sure. Her house looked very well maintained, so I wondered if she had a husband to take care of things.

One wintery morning, we got lucky. Near the top of the hill, we caught sight of her scraping frost off the windshield of her Volvo. Warmth spread through me, despite the chilly air. I did not know what to say. I was like a teenager in the presence of his first love.

"Hi Ruth!" Sam shouted out, saving me from further embarrassment.

Her face lit up, as did my heart.

"Hello boys! What are you doing outside on such a cold morning?" Without giving us the chance to answer, she continued, "Would you like to come in for coffee and hot chocolate?"

After several awkward moments, I found my words.

"I thought you'd never ask!"

We sat at her living room and enjoyed the warming beverages. Ruth's company was far more warming though.

She is beautiful.

After a little conversation about the neighborhood and this and that, Ruth asked, "Have you ever been married, Johann?"

"Never," I replied shaking my head slowly. "I had several dear relationships, though," I added to reduce my answer's negativity.

"How about you, Ruth? You're a beautiful woman.... I'm sure you've had many opportunities."

"Well … oh, thank you," she replied with an attractive modesty. "Yes, I had many chances for marriage since I came to America, but did not take any of them." She sank into her thoughts then smiled. "*C'est la vie* … no regrets."

The atmosphere changed.

"I am sorry if my question…."

"No, Johann. That's quite alright." She took my hand in hers and my heart quickened. "I just had a dark chapter in my life. We all do."

I said nothing. Instead I looked at her but her eyes had gone elsewhere. Only after a painful silence did she return her eyes to mine.

"You probably saw the Menorah in my window."

"Yes, I did."

"I was in Poland during the war…. I am Jewish, Johann."

My mouth became dry and my heart raced. Ugly images came before me as the room seemed to spin. I tried to stand but my legs would not comply. I heard Ruth asking if I felt alright but my efforts to reply failed.

Ruth … a name from a work camp – the one I was in charge of. But….

I grabbed the armrests and made another attempt to stand. Then came the blessed darkness….

"Johann? Do you hear me?"

Ruth's soft voice haunted my mind as I slowly rose out of unconsciousness. My eyes opened and in time I saw Ruth's worried face.

"Can you hear me now, Johann?"

"Yes," I whispered slowly.

"How do you feel? Try to relax and don't try to do too much."

She dabbed my forehead with a cool, moist cloth. I closed my eyes, enjoying her touch. Then I felt smaller hands on my face.

"Are you going to the hospital too?" little Samuel asked worriedly.

I smiled as much as I could.

"No, my friend. I'll be fine. It's just a little dizziness – no need for a hospital."

Relieved, he hugged me.

"This little guy really loves you. Such a rare and wonderful thing to see such strong love between friends."

"Yes, I'm quite lucky."

I turned to Samuel.

"I love you, little guy – with all my heart."

"I am sorry to cause you this trouble. We'll be off as soon as I am up."

"I'll take you home – I insist."

I did not argue. Soon enough I was able to stand and Ruth drove us home. Anne was just arriving. Ruth and I sat in my living room.

"Better now?"

"Well, I am no longer dizzy, a beautiful lady is keeping me company ... how do you think I feel?" My laugh answered my own question. "I don't want this day to end."

"A nice answer.... It seems I can leave you then."

"No, please stay a while longer," I all but pleaded.

She looked at me seriously.

"What happened back at my house, Johann? Why did you pass out when I mentioned the Holocaust?"

"I felt a bit weak since this morning," I quickly answered, hoping my face did not betray dishonesty.

She nodded but I doubt she believed me.

"I was in a work camp called Treblinka," she quickly added.

I commanded Treblinka I from December 1942 until December 1943. Though a work camp, thousands of Jews died there from exhaustion and summary executions.

"I was married then – it lasted but a few months."

I stared at her in disbelief, unable to move. She looked at me carefully.

"He was my high school sweetheart, the love of my life. After six months in the labor camp, he proposed." She released a long sigh. "I accepted and we were married there in the camp. A rabbi from Lvov presided."

She looked out the window, deep in thought. The sunset cast an orange glow on the trees.

"See, the beauty of the world continues even after all of those horrors. People were humiliated, abused and murdered – and the same sun rose regularly every morning, spreading joy to those who still lived, ignoring the plight of millions." She shook her head slowly. "I could never understand that...."

Tears formed in her eyes. My heart was in pain. I wanted to help her, I wanted to hug her. But how could I? I was one of her nightmares.

"I am sorry to hear that," I eventually managed to say.

"I am sorry to bother you with my stories, Johann. You need to rest now."

"No, no. I'd like to hear more," I said determinedly.

I truly wanted to hear her story. I wanted to know what she had experienced. I wanted to know everything about her life – painful though it would be for both of us.

"Are you sure?"

I nodded.

I'm falling in love with her.

"We were married on a magnificent summer night ... yes, under these same skies. I was nineteen years old then. The ceremony was simple and quick, with only my parents and a half dozen friends present, but of course it was very special for us. We did not want to lose the hope of life.... It was a mistake."

I instinctively wanted to say she was wrong, but I did not want to interrupt the flow of her memories and end a moving experience.

"What no one knew was that I was pregnant when we got married."

She gauged my reaction. I did not blink. Her gaze returned to the window and to the past.

"Four months later I gave a birth to a beautiful baby girl. I named her Sara – my mother's name."

A spark of memory briefly illuminated memories within me. But I pushed them to the side and focused on her story.

"Ruth ... please go on."

"We hid the baby girl for a couple of months. We hoped the war would be over soon and we would be liberated. Almost every day there were rumors to that effect. Since my parents also lived with us, we all had hope."

"Until that day when a new officer arrived. Schaffer was his name. He was a *monster*."

I gulped down water to stave off another bout of dizziness.

Schaffer was an assistant. I remembered when he arrived from Berlin where he had been highly recommended as a fiercely dedicated officer who knew how to handle such camps. He firmly believed in the Final Solution and had creative ideas on expediting the process. Such people were prized in those days.

There was more in my memory of a "Ruth" and a "Sara," but it eluded me just then. There were thousands of people in these camps. Hundreds of thousands. Millions.

"Next day, they conducted a selection," she continued expressionlessly. "Do you know that term?"

"I've ... I've come across it."

"They conducted one every so often to determine who was still good for work. Those too old, sick or exhausted ... were sent to Treblinka II. That was a death camp not far away."

"I know," I said.

I immediately regretted my words. Whatever went through her mind was not conveyed on her expression. She continued.

"In that selection, they did something new. They searched our barracks – Schaffer in the lead. Maybe he wanted to show his presence to his soldiers or maybe he was just a monster. My husband's father and mother were healthy and capable of work, but Schaffer decided they were too old – the Treblinka II group. When they protested he pulled his pistol and shot them. First he shot the father. The mother, who was in the group of women, ran in tears to her husband's body. He shot her also. Her body fell on her husband's and they remained there. My husband was in shock. His parents ... gone ... killed ... in less than a minute."

Schaffer's pistol ... a P-38.... I was there.

A painful memory came to me, like a bayonet thrust. My head hurt severely and I refused to accept it. Panic started to take hold. That was the missing information. I began to put together the pieces.

"Then it was the old people's turn. Many of them were simply killed without any determination as to their fitness. He enjoyed killing Jews, just for the fun of it."

I arrived later that day for a spot inspection – part of my duty to ensure timely production of war materiel. I did not like summary executions. They upset the daily routine, caused delays and brought fear to the workforce. Most of all they needlessly reduced the prisoner count.

"My mother and father were lucky that day. They were murdered later though, in the gas chambers of Treblinka II."

I recalled the day and her account gave it new life, right in front of my eyes.

I know what's coming.

"We heard one of the Ukrainian soldiers shout out from the barracks. He brought a bundle to the officer. I realized, to my horror, what he held in his hand."

I know....

"It was my baby ... it was Sara."

I know....

*   *   *

I was just getting out of my staff car on my way to the scene when I saw Schaffer holding something amid several Ukrainian soldiers. I heard a woman scream as she ran towards Schaffer flailing her hands frantically. I increased my pace and pulled my black SS cap down tightly on my head to keep it from blowing off. Two SS soldiers held the woman then Schaffer tossed the bundle in the air, aimed his P-38 and fired into it.

The woman shrieked uncontrollably as three pops sounded.

I started to run. Schaffer then leveled his pistol at the woman.

"Halt!" I shouted. "Halt!"

Schaffer did not seem to hear me. I pulled my pistol and fired into the air. He noticed me then.

As I reached the group they all promptly saluted, even Schaffer.

"Hauptsturmführer Schaffer, what is the meaning of this?"
My face was red.

"Nothing serious, Herr Oberführer . . ." Schaffer smiled, revealing his stained, horse-like teeth. "I'm just about to kill this Jewess."

I looked at the woman. Her mouth was still open in an endless scream, a scream that would never end. She started to tremble.

"Why, may I ask, are you about to shoot this woman?" I asked sternly.

"She screamed," he responded matter-of-factly, then laughed. The other soldiers around joined his laughter until they saw I was not engaging in the levity.

"And why did she scream?"

"She was hiding a baby in the barracks. We found it and I killed it."

He pointed to the bloodstained bundle atop a pile of discarded inmate uniforms.

Such incidents were not uncommon yet this scene was different, though I could not have articulated why that day. Maybe I had seen so many and did not want to see any more. Maybe I already disliked Schaffer as one who paid more attention to personal hatreds than to war needs. Or maybe something happened that day. All I know is that seeing the agonized, broken mother tripped something inside me.

I paced back and forth, trying to control my rage. Without warning, I approached Schaffer, pulled my pistol and pressed it hard against his temple. He was stunned. Fear filled his face.

"How does this feel, Hauptsturmführer?" I spat out. "You enjoy screams, eh. Do you want to scream for us now? Come now, Hauptsturmführer. Give us all a good scream to enjoy."

The Ukrainians stood by, respecting my superior rank, though I'm sure they were confused. I had developed a way of handling these situations.

"This camp has schedules – which we shall all endeavor to meet!"

Every word was stressed, almost hissed. I confess I enjoyed humiliating this loathsome officer – a churl who had been given power only due to the war.

"This camp – *my* camp – has to produce materiel for our army. Does anyone not understand this?"

I looked around. The soldiers all nodded in awe. A uniform and rank can have that effect on some men. I smashed my pistol across Schaffer's face as hard as I could, breaking his nose. He groaned as he fell.

I turned my attention to the underlings.

"Treblinka II is for extermination ... and they are doing an excellent job there, I can assure you. Our job is to produce gravel for our roads and that is precisely what we will do."

I glared at one sergeant to make my point clear – and my authority unquestioned. "Do you have objections, Scharführer Müller? Or have you decided that you have a better grasp on the war than Berlin does?"

Müller jolted to attention and exclaimed, "Nein, Herr Oberführer."

Satisfied that my position was not in question, I continued berating them.

"No more summary executions – none! No women, no children, no one. It reduces our count. Is this understood?"

The soldiers responded crisply in the affirmative. Boots clicked.

So obedient ... too obedient.

"Someone help him to the infirmary," I mumbled as I turned away.

I remembered looking at the broken soul of a mother who now looked at me with uncertainty.

I should have allowed him to kill her ... better for her. She's unlikely to survive now anyway. She's lost everything. They fall into despair, their work declines....

If I had arrived a minute earlier today, I could have saved her baby.

Bah! Who am I deceiving? This is not my decision or my army or my bureaucracy or my Reich. I am just a soldier – one who obeys orders.

If I had arrived a minute earlier today,

The mother lay on the ground, weeping and confused.

"What is your name?" I asked.

She slowly raised her eyes to reveal a dirty face on which tears had formed paths all the way down her cheeks.

"Ruth," she replied amid quiet sobs.

"And the baby's name?"

Something made me want to know the child's name. Maybe I thought that knowing it would give it life of some sort.

"Sara...."

The woman's desperate eyes reflected a soul that had undergone unbearable pain – the pain of losing a baby. I felt sorry for her and wanted to help her. I wanted to save her from what almost assuredly lay in store. Then I looked about at the machinery of death surrounding us.

I cannot do anything. Not for her, not for others.

"Go back to work, Ruth. We have schedules to meet," I told her quietly.

She knew that I had saved her. She seemed to comprehend that I had to be harsh in front of the other soldiers but that I was unlike them. She slowly nodded and stumbled back to her group. My head slumped in shame. Shame from my soul's insistence that I do more and my mind's judgment that I could not.

I did not like it that her eyes had looked so penetratingly into mine.

*　　　*　　　*

Now those eyes were in front of me, a quarter century afterwards, thousands of miles away, but under the same skies.

Some force ... has caused our paths to cross again.

"And that is how I lost ... my baby girl."

Her words and my memory – a powerful and surreal retelling of a tragedy. The details matched in horrifying detail.

"I am so sorry, Ruth," I added in a soft voice that hid my emotion.

Neither of us spoke. The sun had set and the room was getting dark and chilly.

Captivated in my memories, I mumbled, "If I had arrived earlier...."

"What?" she asked in puzzlement.

It took a few seconds to realize what I had said. I looked at her with great discomfort.

"I am so very sorry for your loss, Ruth."

I don't think she thought anything of it.

"My husband was murdered a week later, by Schaffer. The higher officer was not there to save him. Well," she laughed bitterly, "he could not be there all the time and save all of us. In any event, he was one of them."

I did not say anything. How could I?

We sat there awhile. She with her thoughts, I with mine.

"Well! I'm so sorry to burden you with my gloomy recollections. How do you feel, Johann? Maybe a cup of tea?"

"Tea would be quite nice, thank you."

I did not want her to leave. I wanted to be with her and wanted to hear more of her life, but it was getting late and I knew that this would have to wait. Enough for one night.

Our paths crossed again. But why?

I thought how absurd our situation was. The work camp commander and the work camp prisoner. She said it herself, I was one of them. I looked at her delicate face as the vanishing sun cast its last light on her. Yes, it was she. Ruth was of course younger and emaciated then, but the facial features were there. The same proud cheek bones, beautiful eyes, fullness of hair, and petite nose. I knew she could not recognize me as my face had been surgically altered. She probably thinks that I'm an amiable pensioner.

"Another thing...."

She was back in her past as she sipped her tea.

"That higher-ranking officer, the camp commander ... he was different. I sensed he did not like the junior officer. The way he looked at me ... the way he talked to me. I sensed ... regret ... that if he could have prevented Sara's death, he would have."

I said not one word but my heart was shouting out in jubilation.

We did not talk much about this topic after that. In other conversations she mentioned that she never remarried. After the war she did not want to have a family. After the labor camp, she was sent to another work camp, near Auschwitz, which was liberated as her health was failing and she would have been sent to Birkenau. After months in a DP camp, she moved to the United States where her cousins had fled before the war. But she preferred to be alone.

She loves Webster.

We spent time together almost every day. Daytimes meant walks with Samuel and conversations with Ruth. We never crossed beyond the line of basic friendship. She had her wall, I had my own. I think that we were in love with each other but could not push our relationship into romance.

I tried to get used to the idea that I would never be able to tell her about me. She asked a few times about my past and I responded with my alibi of a business in Switzerland. That seemed to suffice. She never probed into my past and I did not encourage her to do so.

We went to Cape Cod from time to time and spent many wonderful weekends there, walking on the broad beaches, taking in the salty air and looking at the ships on the horizon. Maybe we liked the Cape because it stood for new paths and quaint innocence. The limitless ocean gave the feeling of universal goodness – the goodness that left us in the past returned to us just to prove it was still there. We both lived in the moment and it was a beautiful moment.

One day, while strolling through Chatham, she mentioned a desire to go to Israel.

"There is a Holocaust museum there called *Yad Vashem*. Will you come with me?"

Israel

ESPITE MY NEW NAME and face, I dreaded visiting Israel – a country all but established by Holocaust survivors. The people there would consider me a criminal and as someone to be brought to account. Over the years I had read a great deal about Israel and I must say that I gained great respect for it. The Jews had struggled against all odds and established a country of their own, then defended it from surrounding countries that vastly outnumbered them.

Imagine the Nazis seeing this.

I remembered the propaganda so well. The Jews contribute nothing. They are mere parasites who live off of others. They have no future. Well, I've lived to see that as nonsense. They have a country of their own now, with technology, science, arts, and a military. They have built a modern society that lives alongside age-old beliefs. I salute them.

Still, to them I am a criminal – in the same category as Eichmann and deserving of the same fate.

Many times I politely declined Ruth's invitation or deflected the issue, but eventually I agreed. I actually wanted to see the Jewish homeland. I wanted to see what the survivors had built with their own hands. If they were to recognize me and put me to trial … well, it might be just. I was willing to die to see Israel.

Ruth was very happy she wouldn't be going to Israel alone. She wanted to experience the country and especially the Yad Vashem museum with her best friend. She could not have picked a more suitable person, though of course she did not know that.

She arranged everything and on one warm day in August we flew to Israel. We landed in Tel Aviv's airport in the afternoon and took a taxi to our hotel in Jerusalem, about fifty miles away.

"What beautiful views of the ancient city! What do you think, Johann?"

I looked at the modern built side-by-side with the ancient, and was amazed. I was proud of the country, almost as though it were my own. Hard work and ingenuity are appreciated in all cultures.

Ruth had done an extraordinary amount of homework and knew exactly where we should go. We visited the Western Wall, sometimes known as the Wailing Wall, which is a sacred edifice for Jews, as it is the remaining part of the wall that surrounded the Temple. Astounding. Many orthodox rabbis and their students were there, praying and conducting religious ceremonies.

The marketplace, the old city and the new city as well were breathtaking. The city, indeed the whole country, was a monument of triumph over Nazism. I found this a pleasant thought.

On the fifth day we went to the Yad Vashem, the Holocaust museum. Taking in the sights of ancient buildings and glittering new ones is quite different from looking into the face of evil.

I had learned to distance myself from my memories. This often happens as the years roll by. But time can help in denial – pushing everything aside and telling us we were not there or that it was someone else's fault. Time allowed me to see myself as a mere observer to distant events. After all, a Swiss pensioner had nothing to do with Germany or the Reich or the SS or Treblinka.

Ruth and I walked hand in hand through the museum – more for support than from affection. Not many words were spoken. I recognized many places in the pictures on display. I remembered the camps, I remembered the landscape and I even recognized some of the officers. I had dined with a couple of them.

The photographs of children, the elderly and others were on every wall, in sobering black and white enlargements. Piles of bodies in grotesque sprawls. It was everywhere, all around me, and did not leave me any escape. Then there were artifacts – immense piles of glasses, clothing, combs....

A woman in her forties stood before a photograph of a few children looking into the camera. She remained there looking carefully at the image. She turned to me all of a sudden and pointed to the photograph.

"That's me ... that's me."

"You?" I asked as I pointed to the photo.

"Yes, that is certainly me. I can't believe it.... They have a picture of me here."

She smiled bravely.

Ruth was intrigued. "You should tell this to someone here. They would very much like to document your stories for the archives."

They'd be glad to document some of mine.

As I continued to ponder this I thought I should accept a trial. I heard about Eichmann's capture and trial. I never met him but heard about him quite often. After all, he directed the transportation system that brought Jews into the camps. I think he deserved execution as did Schaffer. Both were vicious, cruel men.

Well, I deserve the same fate. Although I never shot or killed people myself, I was in charge of people who did. And that is what matters.

"You look German," the woman said.

I was deep in my thoughts and it took a while to form a response.

"I am Swiss, madam," I answered politely.

"I do not know why, but to me you look German," she insisted.

"My ancestors were from Germany, but they emigrated to Switzerland long ago."

My manners were impeccable, though the veracity of my statements was not.

"Well ... perhaps. You nonetheless look very German."

She seemed almost antagonistic. Ruth looked cautiously at her then at me, eager to ease the tension.

"I am sure she has gone through a lot. She is not herself just now."

"Actually, she is," I heard myself say.

A wish to see myself punished was at play, I'm sure – as it had been in other times when I let a word slip out. Ruth looked at me. I searched her eyes for a reaction.

"I have relatives that were Germans. What to do – I have German blood in me."

"True enough," she responded. "Almost everyone I know has some German ancestry."

She turned back to the photograph and began to tell her story.

"I remember that day well. It was the day of relocation for us kids. I was almost eight years old and my brother David here," she pointed towards a younger child, "was six. We were about to leave for a new camp – or so they said."

She laughed dryly and bitterly.

"They killed most of them."

Her words chilled me. I did not want to hear any more but she had already returned to her grim narrative – testimonial from a Holocaust survivor.

"The picture here was for Red Cross representatives who inspected our camp. See – we are dressed reasonably well. They fixed our rooms and even prepared a play area. They served us fresh bread that morning and gave each of us an apple. You never forget those little things. They said that after the inspection we would be going to another camp ... to be with our parents. We were all happy that day."

She pointed again towards the picture.

"See, if you look carefully you'll see that some of the children's faces are not so sad. They had a good morning and developed some hope ... a false hope ... the falsest of hopes."

The story was now captivating me.

"After that day … we were taken to a big hall for the night. Without any food or water they put us on a train in the next morning.…"

She paused. Ruth put an arm around her.

"You have to understand that for children, there is no sense of time. We did not know for how long we would be on that train. They packed us in a cattle car. We were all standing as they hauled us like animals to someplace or another. It was a hot summer and everyone was very thirsty. The older children – ten or twelve – helped the young ones. The children had to relieve themselves and some vomited due to the heat and the rocking back and forth of the train. Very quickly there was a horrible stench in the cars. Some of the children cried for their mothers. Some became exhausted and sat in the filth.

"With every stop, we poked our fingers outside the openings and pleaded for water. Poking our fingers out – that was the idea of one of the older children. 'Maybe if we stick our little fingers out and cry for water, there will be good people to splash us with water.' We traveled through many villages and towns and could see hundreds of people through the openings, but none of them gave us water.

"Just when we almost gave up, the train stopped near a dairy farm. We could hear and smell the cows. We saw a peasant woman walking nearby. We started to plead for water and shoved our little fingers out into the air. The woman heard us and came to the car.

"She became quite angry. 'What kind of monsters do such thing? Wait, my little ones. I'll try to open the car and get you out.'

"We had hope but some of us knew the guards would see her soon. She brought buckets of water and splashed them across the car's exterior. That was the most refreshing water I've ever had. We moistened our lips with joy and tried to catch as much water as we could. For a short while, we were children again.

"We heard the peasant woman moving towards the front. Then we heard soldiers yelling at her. We saw two soldiers roughly escorting her back to her farm as she yelled back at them about their cruelty to children. I'll never forget that woman. I think she was German – perhaps that is why they did not beat her or kill her."

She stopped and wiped tears from her eyes.

"I protected my little brother all the time. He was a good boy. He did not complain even when hungry or thirsty. He did not complain when he was hot and he did not complain when I told him that I did not have toilet paper to help him with his potty. He sat the whole time in my arms and from time to time asked, 'Are we going to see mom and dad soon ... as they promised?' I had hope, I suppose. But deep inside I knew we would not see them again. I wanted to encourage him but I did not want to lie to him either. I am against lies of any kind."

She looked at us, as though for prompting to continue. Our expressions sufficed.

"We had to endure several more days without food or water. Some good people threw water on us here and there. Many children passed out from exhaustion and some never woke up.

"We arrived at our destination at night. I later learned we were at Auschwitz. They took us out of the train and arranged us in rows, probably for counting. At least we were out of that horrible train. I remember the soldiers shouting commands. My brother and I were tired and just wanted to go to our new barracks to sleep. We stood in silence as we heard the soldiers talking, then we were told to sit on the ground.

"One of the children started to talk with the others and we strained to hear. He said he knew German and that they were going to get rid of us immediately. We'd be marched to a pit outside the camp and there they would shoot us all."

She wiped her glasses and composed herself. We waited patiently.

I knew about the mass graves. I knew about marching groups of people out of the camp and then shooting them along the rim of a pit. Sometimes they dug the pits. Sometimes we used antitank ditches made by the Polish army before the war.

"Children can be creative when they feel endangered, sometimes even more so than adults."

A small smile appeared on her face.

"We were not about to give up that easily. After the boy listened more and confirmed what was to happen, we decided that we would not go to death as simply as that. We had to do something.

"So we made a plan. As we marched outside the camp towards the mass graves, just as any of us saw a wooded area where we could hide, a signal would be given. First we will run at the soldiers – all two hundred or so of us – and knock into them with as much force as our tired little bodies could muster. This will stun them, maybe even knock them down or make them drop their guns. Then, in the dark confusion, we would race for the woods. We knew that if we all simply ran towards the woods, we would be easy targets and mowed down like grass. But if we attacked first, it would buy us some precious time that could make the difference – children's logic in dark times."

The woman looked at us.

"What do you think? Were we right? A good plan?"

"Yes, a sound plan … in dark times," I said in a low voice.

It was terrible to think about a group of children running for their lives in the dark while soldiers fired at them.

I miss Samuel.

"As we walked outside the camp, a couple of children called out, 'Look there! Woods!' – our moment had come. 'I want you with me at all times,' I told David. 'You stick to me like glue.' He nodded and I could feel adrenalin rush through me. There was a second of silence as we waited for someone to start our assault. Then one of the older children shouted, 'Attack!' and we rushed the solders as we cried out at the top of our little lungs. The soldiers were stunned and did not have time to aim their guns as we swarmed upon them. Many of them fell to the ground so we ran for the forest. The trees looked dark and threatening in the night but that night they beckoned us warmly as a hiding place, protection … life.

"David and I ran amid many other children and I thought this gave us protection from what was surely to come. Soon enough, we heard the soldiers' guns as they fired upon the little moving targets. I saw many children fall. 'Faster, faster– towards the trees there,' I shouted to David. He panted heavily and I could hear his lungs whistling as we raced for the woods.

"I could hear the soldiers shouting in confusion and running about in the dark. Concern about shooting fellow soldiers probably limited the fire brought down on us. Had one of the older children counted on that? Still we could hear gunfire cracking behind us and bullets whistling overhead.

" 'Quick – the trees to the left ... we are almost there,' I told David. Many children had already vanished into the deep woods. The soldiers would conduct searches in the morning – we were sure of that.

"And then I heard a thump, like the sound of a stone hitting a pond surface. David's hand became heavy as his feet began to fail him. 'Don't stop now,' I insisted."

The woman's voice broke and she started to cry. Ruth hugged her and I held her hand. It was heartbreaking to imagine two children, brother and sister, running for their lives as soldiers fired upon them – and the young one being hit by a bullet.

"He gathered all of his strength, little David did, and he continued to run like a little devil.... Poor boy ... poor little boy."

She smiled bravely.

"We ran blindly into the woods. The foliage scratched and cut us. Nothing could stop us, we were free. We ran until we reached the tall trees. David's hands became heavy again but I felt safe. 'We can stop now,' I told him.... He did not answer.

"I found some soft grass and we lay down on it. I pulled some branches and leaves on us to provide warmth and hide us from animals ... and from soldiers.

" 'How do you feel?' I asked my little brother. 'Where did you get hurt?' He murmured that he felt something on his back. I felt along his back and ... the fear of all worlds grabbed me. His shirt was soaked with blood. `Oh, no!' I whispered in growing panic. 'I do not feel any pain,' he bravely replied as his little hand held mine. 'I'm just very cold.' He began to shake. I held him close – the best way to give warmth that night. 'Are you better?' I whispered. 'Yes, much better, thanks.'

"His shaking stopped and we lay there in the night, listening to the forest sounds. They were like music to us after the ordeal of the last few days. 'Where are the stars?' asked David. 'The trees are hiding them,' I answered. I searched the tree cover and found an opening to the heavens. 'There! Look there! You can see stars.' He hugged me more tightly. `You're right. I can see stars.' I was happy for that.

"Then he told me, 'Thank you for showing me the stars.' I laughed quietly. 'Of course, you silly boy. I love to see them also. Now go to sleep and in the morning we will search the woods for partisans. Maybe they can help us.' He nodded and snuggled in my arms. I kissed his forehead. We both fell asleep very quickly."

She paused to gather herself.

"The early morning cold woke me up. David lay in my arms with a beautiful smile on his face. I tried to wake him up but he would not open his eyes. I nudged him and called his name, but it did not help. His body was cold. David lay there – a smiling angel."

We were all in tears … and in reverent silence.

"That's how I lost my little brother David. I find comfort in knowing that at least he did not feel any pain. He died in his sleep, as we hugged each other beneath the stars. What do you think?"

"You are certainly right … of course."

I hurried my soft reply so that my voice would not break.

"I was not aware of the wound's severity. I arranged his clothes and laid him on the bush with his face towards the skies, so he could see the stars – the stars that meant joy and freedom. In the camp every night, he fell asleep looking at the stars. He asked me once, why people were not like stars? When I asked him what he meant, he answered, 'Nice, bright and shiny.…' He is with the stars now."

She stood up to leave us.

"I have to go now. It was good meeting you both, and thank you for listening to my memories."

"Wait," Ruth gently held her hand "What is the end of the story? How were you saved?"

"Oh yes.… It's not that important.… I found a partisan band and stayed with them. There were many children with them and we helped them to fight the Nazis in many ways – gathering firewood, foraging for food, treating wounds.…

"After the war I went to New York. I always wanted to go to

America as a child. I thought that it would give me a reason for life – a new life. I opened a clothing business and prospered. I had everything – a big home, cars and money. But I never recovered. After the Holocaust and all I had gone through, I keep waiting for all this to end.... I never got married and never had children."

She smiled one last time to us.

"I am just waiting for life to end."

She started to walk away, but it was my time to ask one last question.

"Madam ... please. May I know your name?"

"Evelyn," came her only reply.

We looked after her silently, a small figure of a lady who had survived the Holocaust. At least part of her had. I think part of her was still in that forest with her little brother.

Love

T HE MOOD OF OUR trip changed after that day in the Yad
Vashem museum. Very much for the worse. Neither of us
could appreciate the country's beauty anymore and we lost our
passion to travel in it. We had planned for several more days in Israel
but we rescheduled a return flight for an earlier date.

We hardly talked as we flew across the Atlantic. The museum visit
had opened old wounds that left us with deep sadness. Upon reaching
Webster I spent several days in bed. I did not want to wake up in the
morning. I did not want to wake up at all.

Something pulled me out of my profound depression. Something
wonderful and unique and loving.

On the fourth day Anne and Sam arrived and announced that
while I was away Samuel had made a gift for me – a Rosh Hashanah
gift. Sam beamed as he presented me a small clay apple with a silver
spoon that he had diligently made at daycare. I expressed my loving
gratitude with a lengthy hug.

"I am a bit jealous that he made this for you not me," Anne
admitted, partly in jest.

We both knew that Samuel loved to make things there – and more
often than not they were for me.

"Oh stop complaining!" I quipped. "You have the high privilege
of being his mother and the recipient of a very special love."

Sam beamed at Anne. He knew just what I was talking about.

I was so happy to see him that my mood perked up immediately.

"What is this? You've grown an inch since I saw you – maybe two!"

"I missed you," he exclaimed.

"And you know I missed you as well, my little craftsman," I replied as I tousled his hair.

Anne looked at us quietly. "I never saw such a connection like you two have.... Anyway off to work I go. Have a pleasant day, gentlemen."

"Thanks, Anne – you too."

Just as I was formulating plans for the day, my friend offered advice.

"Johann, let's go for our morning walk."

"Yes. We'll see how Ruth's doing."

Ruth and I hadn't spoken since the return and I more than suspected that she too was mired in gloom. We needed to get her out of her miserable memories. Samuel had just saved me. We would save Ruth.

Mitzvah.

I packed some fruit and in no time we were ambling down the lane.

"We're off to see Ruth ... she needs us...."

Samuel looked up with a puzzled look.

"You'll understand better when you grow up," was the best answer I had.

Ruth looked downcast as she opened the door for us, though her face immediately lit up on seeing us. That heartened me and set the stage for a lovely time. We shared a light snack along with the tea she always had not far from the kettle. A little conversation and Sam's exuberance brightened her day. An hour or so later, as Sam noted a need to head back, Ruth was truly sorry the visit was coming to an end.

Our routine had returned. Every day I picked up Samuel from daycare and he stayed with me until evening. Sometimes our late afternoon constitutionals were done in twilight – often in the dark. Samuel loved to light the way with his flashlight.

We visited Ruth and she visited us as well. Many nights Ruth and I had evening dinners. She knew several cuisines, even German, and did them all quite well. I learned to enjoy Jewish food. My favorite was the latkes she made on Hanukkah – wonderful with sauerkraut and cream cheese. We strolled through the neighborhood and talked about many subjects. We never discussed the war years though. She did not want to talk about it and I did nothing to raise the matter.

"What's in the past, let it stay in the past," she once said – and I agreed.

She met Anne and Elliot and became another friend of the family. Anne told me many times that Ruth and I were a wonderful couple and that I should make the relationship a closer one. I told Anne that it was still too soon – an excuse, of course. I loved Ruth but had my own reservations about drawing closer. I hoped that with time I'd overcome them.

Whatever feelings I had for Ruth – and there were many warm ones – guilt was never far from the surface. My past … her baby … my failure to intervene. Every time I looked at her lovely face, my heart sank a bit. We sometimes spent the night at the other's home, but never shared the same bedroom.

Nonetheless, I loved her with all my heart.

One night she and I were sitting on my front porch. Anne had just picked Sam up after the three of us had been for a long walk to the lake, where we had skimmed stones across the glass-like surface. We sat on our rocking chairs like old people and enjoyed the last beams of the sun that, though set, was still sending a beautiful glow into the darkening skies above the horizon.

"That little boy has worn me out," Ruth exclaimed. "He ran all over the place!"

"I thought we'd never keep up," I added as we returned to our appreciation of the skies.

"I love it like this…."

"I love the evening breeze," I added as I took her hand. "And I love spending time with you."

Before I even finished my sentence I realized I had given an opening that no woman would ever turn down.

"Yet, nothing has happened between us," she added with both humor and ruefulness.

"What do you mean?"

I know full well.

"We travelled everywhere, even overseas, we sleep at each other's home quite often, yet no romance has blossomed. They don't just blossom. People make them blossom."

She looked into my eyes, searching for an answer. I turned back to the horizon.

"Why not, Johann? Why haven't we made our relationship into something more?"

I looked at her silently, unable to summon anything near the courage required.

"Why not, Johann?" she repeated. "Why are we not ... a couple? A true couple? Is it religion? I've already told you that traditional customs mean little to me."

She held my hand.

"I look into people's hearts. You are a good man. I sensed it from the beginning ... as though I long knew it anyway.... Is religion an issue with you?"

Irony can be cruel.

The sunset was almost over and the darkness was winning out. Knowing she could no longer see my eyes and what they said and what they might be hiding, I found words.

"Religion is not important to me.... I love you, Ruth.... But there are things I cannot tell you."

"Everyone has things packed away, but it's no reason for our not being together. You'll tell me with time ... I am in a no rush."

I smiled briefly.

"No Ruth. There are things that I am not proud of – things I cannot tell you about ... ever. Not in any amount of time in the world."

She released a long sigh and looked into the dark. The night had taken over completely. The skies filled with sparkling stars and a crescent moon, gently glowing in their silver and white.

"What can be so terrible that you can't tell me, Johann?"

She slid her rocking chair nearer to mine.

"We talk about everything … what can be so secretive?"

You can't imagine.

She just looked at me and released a long sigh. I looked out into the unresponding night.

The Fatherland

I THOUGHT ABOUT GOING back to Germany. Not to live permanently, just for a visit. It was 1970 and I'd read about the recovery from the ravages of World War Two –the "economic miracle" as it was called. I wanted to visit my hometown of Hamburg. I also wanted to see Berlin where I was stationed at times. Is where the Third Reich began and ended. It is where Plan O went into motion as the Russians closed in.

For many years I had been afraid to go for fear of being exposed. There might be something or someone from my past lurking back there to pull me in. But still, I wanted to return. I came from there. Yes, a different era and a long time ago, but it was my home. The woman at the holocaust museum in Israel said I looked German. Well, I *am* German.

There were many immigrants in America who yearned to go back to Hungary or Italy. I was hardly an immigrant as Americans thought of that term. I wasn't fleeing poverty and seeking opportunity. Nonetheless, I shared their yearnings to go back home someday.

Germany was helping Holocaust survivors who were living in Israel. The German government sent them monthly payments, for the rest of their lives. German ministers proclaimed their lasting friendship with Israel. "Our countries are tied together forever," our chancellor said in a radio speech. "The horrifying crimes of our Nazi past compel us to commit to Israel and to help the Jewish nation for generations to come. We will always ensure the security of the state of

Israel and we will also ensure that no similar crimes against humanity happen again. Not against Jews, not against any other people."

A Boston travel agency set up my flight and lodgings. The TWA flight touched down in Frankfurt and I rented an Audi for the drive up to Hamburg. As I drove inside the city limits I was surprised at the old town's newness. Modern architecture stood gracefully and respectfully aside older structures that had survived the war. Fancy boutiques blended well with quaint neighborhood shops.

The city was much larger than it had been before the war and I no longer knew my way around. I had to hire a taxi to find the neighborhood I grew up in. As we turned off of Hanover Strasse I spied the modest house I was born in. My heart raced in elation. It was still there! It had been remodeled and painted in vibrant colors that no burger of the thirties would have been bold enough to employ.

I hopped out of the cab to walk around and a familiar scent filled my nostrils. I knew that aroma! I grew up with it.

Lilac blossoms!

I closed my eyes to savor them. Our neighbors competed to raise the most gorgeous and aromatic flowers and our block specialized in those violet beauties.

I opened my eyes and saw old, prewar houses that been refashioned in keeping with the times. As in my day, every house was nicely adorned with flowers and trees. Swing sets, bicycles and toys were all about.

It was late morning and the neighborhood seemed almost deserted. The parents were at work, the children at school. Most mothers worked, I gathered. The windows of my old house were graced with azure curtains, and stone planters bursting with violets decorated the ledges. The stonework was still in good shape and the wood trim had been freshly painted in sky blue.

Through the fence I could see my old backyard and I saw myself playing soldiers there with friends. An old tree that once had a swing ... a gravel path that my father had built to the garden. How many times had mother scolded me for trampling over her daffodils? Youthful impetuousness propelled me off the path many a time – and onto mother's unsuspecting flowers. "Stay on the path father made! Why do you think he made it?"

The door swung open and a young woman came out. She was young, in her mid-twenties, with long brown hair.

"Good morning, sir. Do you need help of some sort?"

I flinched. After so many years in hiding, I had to pause to comprehend my native tongue. I had spoken English with the people at the airport and even the cabbie.

"Good morning, madam," I answered in the old language. "I am just looking at your house. By chance, it's the one I grew up in. In fact, I was born here … long ago."

"Ach, I see! My husband and I purchased this house two years ago and we've been redoing it." She was quite pleasant and seemed disposed to help an old man like me.

"You've done wonderful things here!"

"Oh, we love this house. We saved for many years," she replied proudly. "It's remarkable to meet a person born in this house. When was that, may I ask?"

"Oh, many, many years ago," I told her waving my hands at the several decades that had floated off into the air. "You probably weren't even born. It was before the war."

"Oh yes…. Where is your home today?"

"I live in America for many years now. Near Boston. I am a retired Swi … a retired businessman."

"And your family? Are they still here in Germany?"

"No, they passed away a long time ago."

"I'm sorry to hear that."

"I have my own family in America now. They are not blood relatives, but good neighbors who became family."

"Ahhh, so you are not alone. Good."

My German skills were coming back nicely and I was soon talking in the local *Plattdeutsch* manner – an accent my fellow soldiers had found amusing back then.

She leaned over and whispered, "I have a little surprise for my husband when he comes back from work."

I gave her a quizzical look. She put her finger on her mouth as though to keep her words from unseen passersby. We seemed like friends.

"We are going to have a baby – a baby girl!"

Her face brightened in that special way.

"Congratulations!" I exclaimed. "In a way, I am a grandfather to a handsome boy named Samuel. My neighbor's son ... an adorable child."

"So nice to hear. And what brings you back to Hamburg?"

"I wanted to see the old town. After so many years ... oh, I missed it. I wanted to see how it looks today. I wanted to see the changes."

She expected more, I could tell. But of course, I could not tell her more.

"Well, how do you feel about all the changes?"

I took a deep breath and looked around.

"I love it now. It is so lovely ... just as I remembered it in many ways. Of course it is older but the spirit remains."

She remained quiet, hoping to hear more.

"You never forget your childhood," I continued. "I wish I could have stayed a child forever and never grown up."

She laughed and said, "That's what we all want!"

"Yes, but in my case it would have made a world of difference."

She looked puzzled. Or perhaps she thought of my age and made the obvious connection to events before her birth.

"Well, I must be off now. It was my pleasure to meet you, Miss _"

She presented her hand and I gently shook it. I even kissed it in the old manner.

"Schneider, Alena Schneider."

"Alena?" My mind peered well back into the past and I released a long sigh. "I used to know a beautiful young woman named Alena."

I wonder what was her fate....

Tears threatened to erupt from my eyes but I maintained control. Nostalgia can easily turn into weepiness.

"Oh ... and I am Johann Kraus. It has been my pleasure. And I wish you and your family – your growing family – many happy and prosperous years in your house. I had many enjoyable years here."

"Thank you very much," she answered, touched by my well-wishing. "You know, you are more than welcome to join us for dinner if you are in the neighborhood later. My husband would be glad to meet you."

If she would only know who I was....

"Thank you, Alena. But alas I have only three days in the country and I am off for Berlin tonight. Again, it has been my pleasure."

"Enjoy your visit, Johann!"

She drove off on some errands, I suppose, while I remained there with my thoughts. I was happy to know that a charming young family was living in the house that I had grown up in during more innocent days, before the darkness.

I took a taxi back to my car and drove down the autobahn for Berlin.

The autobahn roads were built for the army. Now families drive them for holidays.

I miss Samuel.

The next day, after a hefty breakfast, I went for a long walk through West Berlin. It too was an astonishing sight. When I made my way out of the bunker in 1945, all was in ruins from allied bombs and artillery.

I took a taxi to the Pestalozzistrasse synagogue in the Charlottenburg district. I stood outside in admiration. It was a magnificent edifice, with Judaic symbols and lettering engraved on the front. It was built long ago, before World War One. It had survived Kristallnacht and the ravages of World War Two.

Quite an achievement.

I tentatively went inside and sat for perhaps an hour, watching the people praying quietly. I knew no one there yet I felt I was in a familiar place. I think I found myself praying in some way or another.

As I left I noted that several streets had Jewish names. The city of Berlin now had streets named after Jews. If the Nazis could see it now. A synagogue in the heart of their Reich had outlasted them and the surrounding streets now bore Jewish names. Who would have believed back then that something like this would happen?

That night I watched a political debate that mentioned the laws against Nazism. It is forbidden to preach Nazism in Germany and the issue was not opposed by any of the panclists. That made me happy.

The next day was my last in Berlin. I decided to walk by the old Jewish Museum. I knew it had been shut down by the Nazis but thought it would have been restored and reopened by now. I was disappointed that it had not. Someday, I hope to see it open its doors and become like the Yad Vashem museum in Israel, perhaps with a wooded area outside for children to play in.

As I walked by the old site I noticed two young men, probably college students, heading towards the nearby Berlin Museum.

They are so young.

I was curious.

"Where are you going?" I asked them.

"We are students at the Free University. We are working on a paper about the Holocaust," one answered with the distinct accent of a Berliner, pronouncing many an ending "s" with a "t" and that hard "ch" sound.

They smiled shyly, perhaps because of my age.

"Good to hear," I said. "Johann Kraus is my name and it is nice to meet young people with interests in the past."

"Rudolph, Rudolph Schmidt," said one of them.

"Jacob," said the other "Jacob Cohen. You see, I come from the family of a Holocaust survivor. My father was at Auschwitz. Rudolph here is my best friend. His father was a soldier in the Wehrmacht during the war."

Rudolph spoke up. "We are determined to make sure that such a calamity never recurs. Our friendship symbolizes a truth regarding postwar Germany."

Jacob added, "Our friendship shows that people should never be judged by their race or religion. All people are human beings. All have the right to live in dignity, integrity and peace."

Their interest in the past and hope for the future warmed my heart. This new generation is learning and will not make the mistakes of the past. They will never turn to the Nazi ways. The lessons of those dark years should be taught for generations to come.

"With your permission, I would like to shake the hands of you young men," I said in a quavering voice. "I wish that there had been more like you many years ago."

They smiled proudly and shook my hand. In closing, I wished them success with their research. "Never stop holding to these ideas. Do not let anyone tell you differently." As my emotion built, they began to look at me as though I were a strange but harmless old man. They then entered the old Berlin Museum to work on their project.

It was late afternoon and an invigorating wind came up. As I walked through the half-empty streets I looked at the Berliners going about their day and I felt good. I had the chance to return to the old country and saw that it had changed – completely changed. The Germany of today is a splendid place to live in, raise a family and worship as you please.

A light rain started to fall but I did not care. Happiness flood over me. I walked past another old synagogue where the faithful were gathering. The interior light shone out onto those standing about on the sidewalk. They chatted and laughed before the service began. I heard one member say that his wife was about to give birth any day now.

I stayed on the sidewalk as they entered the synagogue and the service began. The rabbi began with the familiar words that I heard Rabbi Levi intone back in Worcester. I stood there in the drizzle and listened. In the middle of Berlin, not far from where the Final Solution was directed, I stood before a synagogue and listened silently to the comforting sound of Hebrew prayer.

I looked up to the skies and laughed. I poked at the dark clouds and my laughter only grew. I laughed with tears and rain running down my cheeks. I rejoiced because I had my country back. I was proud to be a German again.

In a few hours I'd drive back to the Frankfurt airport and fly back to Boston.

America Again

I RETURNED TO MASSACHUSETTS feeling better about the old country and myself as well. Still, memories occasionally haunted me. As much as I tried to let them go, they lurked inside my soul and came out when they pleased. Although they belong to a distant and receding past, they are still part of my experience. Part of my dark past. They'll be with me the rest of my life.

Ruth was no longer content to remain in the dark. She probed and nudged in every possible way to get information from me. Other times her silence made me think she wanted to put it completely aside. Every now and then I considered telling her the truth and nothing but the truth, as they say, but when it came to doing it ... ahhh, I simply couldn't.

And so we remained best friends, sharing everything – opinions, thoughts and the precious time of each day. We took care of Samuel together, we went for long walks together, we went to synagogue together.

Together as friends, even good friends; but not as lovers, not as husband and wife.

One weekend we went to Cape Cod. We stayed in a Chatham inn near the waterfront where we could wake up to the sounds of seabirds and the roar of the ocean, then stroll along the beach, barefoot, breathing in the ocean air.

We woke up early one especially appealing morning and went for our walk. The skies were crystal clear and the ocean was as smooth and tranquil as it had been since the earth formed. On the horizon skimmed cargo ships on their way to various places around the world. The seagulls made their usual screeches, and lethargic waves caressed our feet. Hand in hand we walked along the empty beach before returning to the inn for a light breakfast.

The inn and its restaurant were a family business that had been passed down over the years. Now Linda ran it. Anne and I had become known there. The cherubic, red-cheeked innkeeper welcomed her frequent guests.

"Good morning, you early love birds."

"Good morning, Linda – and how are you this morning?" Ruth replied.

"Long time no see. Where've you been keeping yourselves?"

"All over the place," I answered casually. "But no place on the Cape has your meals, Linda – especially your breakfasts."

"Oh, we give it our all. Thank you so much, Johann."

Linda always enjoyed our compliments. It was more than obligatory repartee with customers. She liked us. I think she saw something charming in the pair of us.

"You two enjoy your breakfast and your day. It sure looks like it's going to be a beautiful one."

Linda was off to greet the other guests beginning to come in after early walks and late risings.

"I really love her," Ruth said.

"A really sweet woman."

I was eager to get to my sausage and eggs.

We enjoyed our breakfast and then went off to explore a rock formation that boldly shot out into the ocean. We carefully walked to the end of the rocks and found a comfortable spot where we could sit with our feet dangling in the water.

"You know, Johann, I really enjoy our times together."

"As do I. We know how to have fun … for old folks."

We held hands.

"Johann, there is one thing I've had no success in figuring out."

I hope we are not going to revisit that old matter.

"I cannot get rid of the feeling that I know you from somewhere … or at least that I've seen you before."

She looked at me as though trying to decipher a code written across my face.

"I know it makes no sense – I mean, I know that we've never met before … but still. I have an odd feeling that we have."

I smiled softly. Then sadness invaded. I could not imagine my life without her.

I cannot let her know.

"Maybe we did see each other at some point in the past." I gave a mysterious smile as though I possessed a secret. "Maybe in a past life – you know, reincarnation…."

I laughed, she didn't. She scrutinized me even more intently.

"I've seen you somewhere. I just can't point to the time and place. I am sure one day it will pop into my head."

We watched the enormous, timeless ocean – she with her thoughts, I with mine.

Ruth turned to me, gave me an unexpected kiss and boldly said, "Let's get married!"

The astonishment on my face must have amused her.

"What!"

"Why not? We enjoy our time together, we spend our time like a married couple, and many nights we even sleep together … in a way. We mustn't be afraid to move on to the next step – intimacy."

I breathed in heavily. I loved her, of course. But there was simply too much she didn't know and could never understand. I wanted to press her tightly to my heart. I wanted to marry her and provide her anything that she wanted for the rest of her life. I wanted to love her forever but I could not cross that line. And so I fell silent.

"What is it with you?" she asked almost accusingly. "I can see that you love me. Am I not right?"

I remained silent.

"Am I not right, Johann? Do you have feelings towards me?"

"Yes … yes I do."

"What kind, Johann? What kind of feelings do you have towards me?"

What more will she insist on knowing?

"I love you, Ruth," I replied as I met her intent look with my own. "I love you with all my heart – I cannot imagine life without you."

She wiped her tears and grew silent.

"That's what I wanted to hear. That will have to do for now.... I love you too, Johann – with all my heart and soul."

Her words – and my own as well – brought me a flood of joy, like that a young boy feels with his first love. I was happier than I'd been in many years.

Ruth loves me.

She was happy that we both had finally expressed our love for each other. It was a great accomplishment for her. Yes, we both still had miles to go, but I felt that we were moving forward. We shared a real love, and with that came hope...

... and a little impetuousness.

I kissed her. A small peck.

Then we kissed more and more until we were kissing passionately. Two far-from-young lovers, kissing openly along the ocean shore.

We spent the rest of Saturday on the Cape then returned home that evening.

Sunday morning was wet and gloomy. After breakfast I went to Ruth's to help out with her gardening. Despite the drizzle we busily planted seeds and bulbs, which we hoped would bloom spectacularly next spring.

"I love seasonal flowers ... they symbolize joy and celebration for me," Ruth said as we dug a reasonably neat row of holes. "My favorite is the daffodil – pure and aromatic," she added.

"I like to see a colorful blanket of many different flowers," I offered after stopping for a little lemonade. I needed a little break after so much digging in the hard earth which had not softened from what little rain we had had over the last few months. But the earth did not win out and we gently dropped a bulb in each hole and covered them all in. The light rain moistened the soil after a while and created a fresh fecund scent. I breathed it in deeply.

"I love this aroma – lush soil and fresh rain."

Ruth said nothing, leaving a strange silence. She had walked over behind a blueberry tree – not far away, not out of earshot.

Something was wrong.

"Ruth? Are you okay?" I called out as I started off toward the tree. She did not answer. I could see her now, on the ground. I rushed to her.

I spent the night at the hospital while Ruth rested and awaited a series of tests in the morning. A week or so later, the results were in and the news was dreadful. Ruth was diagnosed with ovarian cancer – a late stage of it that had spread into other places, including her spinal column. A tough period was coming for us.

Characteristically, Ruth was not devastated by the news. At times, she was even cheerful.

"If I let this disease destroy my spirits, then I am done for," she used to say. "Better to fight and be happy. That'll give us better odds."

"You're right.... We have to live every day with joy and happiness. We can win."

That winter was a very hard time. I stayed with her as much as I could, day and night. I made an odd sandwich of bologna and cranberries and bowlfuls of chicken noodle soup. Ruth joked that among her people chicken noodle soup was thought to have almost magical powers. The treatments made her weak. She lost so much weight that she looked emaciated. It conjured up an image of her back in Poland.

The thought that she would lose the battle did not cross her mind. As for me, I did not want to think about the worst case. Maybe because of her optimism or maybe because I loved her so much, I simply could not imagine a world without her. I thought her cancer was something that could be controlled, leaving her with many good years ahead. This was a form of denial but one commingled with hope.

Months passed and the treatments had not brightened our prospects. The doctors recommended stopping them. No reason to continue the discomfort that chemotherapy was causing. Better to let things go their way. Ruth had lost the battle.

"Enjoy your time together," the doctor suggested. "Travel … celebrate life. Do not let the sun go down. When the moment comes, we can help you."

Ruth looked worried – more for me.

That night we dined at my home. It was Friday evening and Ruth lit Shabbat candles that illuminated the room with magical hues of yellow and orange. Ruth had made salmon in olive oil and we sat at the table feeling each other out as to how to handle things.

"Johann," she said in a soft voice, "I know it's hard … but remember, if we allow ourselves to get mired in sorrow, we will be wasting precious moments that might otherwise be glorious ones."

"I know.… I just can't help it. A minute, please.…"

She nodded and we collected ourselves before slowly starting on the salmon.

Ruth had accepted the news calmly. I was the one that struggled with disbelief and depression. All she wanted was to spend time together. Samuel had now started first grade. We watched him after school and Ruth helped him with homework. As with my life, he gave greater meaning to hers. He probably helped her stave off bouts of moroseness. I was there to assist, help and support. I had to be strong for her, but I had difficulty eating, sleeping and focusing.

One beautiful April night we lay in my bed and watched the magical stars through my bedroom windows. Ruth lay near me and held my hand. She was warm and soft.

"Johann, I want you to know that you've made my life richer."

I did not want to share the thoughts crossing my mind at that moment.

"From my point of view, we are married," she added.

"Thank you, Ruth … but I do not deserve you."

"No, no. I disagree. I know you better than you think – better than you know yourself. And how in heaven's name can you say something like that? You deserve me and I deserve you. It's called love ... true, eternal love."

I looked at her and realized how happy she was with what we had. No last-minute revelation was going to ruin everything for her. Not now, not at the end. I want to make her happy, especially after my failure long ago.

"Yes ... true, eternal love."

Then she spoke to me as a teacher would to her young student – an esteemed personage insisting on truth.

"You've always been honest with me, so please continue to be so. For the good and for the bad, you were honest and that is what I love in you."

She paused for a moment

"I do not fully know what held back our relationship, but I've respected your position. I assumed that you have a resistance to commitment."

"No," I responded immediately. "That is not the reason."

"Then it was something else ... and I accepted that. I respect your wishes and never want to push you into something you are not ready for."

"Thank you," I mumbled, looking out of the window.

"So please don't change now. Do not do things because of ... what I'm going through."

Silently, I nodded.

"Thank you ... and remember, I love you as you are."

"But do you *know* me?"

My voice was cold. It was the first time she heard me like this and it surprised her.

"Do you *really* know me?" I added.

"Yes, I think I do."

She was standing up to me, though it seemed we were descending into argument.

"No, you don't.... If you did, things would be different ... very different."

She probably thought I was giving her an opening and that this was the time to get things out of me. I was becoming willing to give them to her. I thought it only fair.

"Then tell me – I'm ready. I was ready months ago. You were the one that held back."

The pain and frustration that I kept down over the years were boiling up again. I had never told anyone anything, but now I felt that I could not hold it down anymore. If she understands, then we win. If not, then I lose – everything.

I pressed Ruth to my heart for a while, drawing life and courage. I decided to go ahead ... on faith.

"I am hugging you now because you may not want to hug me anymore after I tell you what I am about to tell you."

She offered me no assurance. I thought that fair and honest. Few things come with assurance.

"I am ready to hear you," she whispered.

I looked at her and thought the entire world was about to change forever. This moment will expose everything that I had held inside since the war. It stayed inside me like a smoldering ember, waiting to erupt into flames. I never thought I'd confess my story to anyone but then again, I never thought that I'd change so drastically that I'd even consider it.

The evil of the Jews ... the master race ... the Final Solution ... the Reich ... its resurgence one day....

How evil, inhuman and cruel we were. I deserve the death penalty – and I was ready for it. For the past years I was mentally prepared to be tried and executed by any court of law. My soul will never be pure again.

Now I would face a judge more just and more wise than found in any court of law. With my heart aching and my eyes near tears, I turned to Ruth.

"I will tell you."

Confession

"**R**UTH … YOU WERE right. We *have* met in the past," I began as my torment built. "Not in good circumstances … very bad ones, in fact. But yes, we've met before."

"Aha," she smiled happily, eager to have it all revealed at last. Feminine ideas of romance must have been racing through her mind. "I knew it! I knew we'd met before."

She awaited my next words, though she could not have expected them.

"It was in the work camp … Treblinka."

"What?" Her eyes became round then quizzical. "You were not in that camp. You're not Jewish – besides I would remember you."

"True, I am not Jewish. There were gypsies there as well – I'm certain of that – but I am not a gypsy. I wasn't an inmate there … nor was I a guard or a kapo."

I had to take a deep breath.

"I was the camp's commander. I commanded Treblinka II."

She remained silent, perhaps realizing that this was going to be a very hard story, for her and for me.

"I don't … How? When?"

A look of partial understanding came across her face.

"Him? The good officer?" she mumbled quietly. "That was you that day? It couldn't...."

"Yes, I commanded Treblinka II," I numbly repeated.

"Have you lost your mind? I clearly remember the commander. His face.... He saved me."

She reacted with solid reasoning, but I could see that she doubted her own thinking and also that fear of what she was learning was beginning to undermine all that she knew and believed and loved.

She chuckled – nervously, I think. It was a way to protect her understanding of me and so much else.

"I do not believe this story, Johann. I just don't. It's too ... it's preposterous."

"Yes, I was – *am* – that man.... But I was too late to save your baby ... and so many others."

My head sank low.

"I am so very sorry, Ruth. But I am that man."

She scrutinized my face, then did the same to the image burned forever into her memory.

"It was a different man, Johann. Stop this nonsense. I'll never forget his face. You look completely different. You are *not* that man."

"Then the plastic surgeon did an excellent job on my face, I would say."

She fell silent then looked at me more closely. I looked at her, hoping for mercy. No – mercy is not the right word. Acceptance maybe.

I took her two hands in mine and sat next to her on the bed.

"I am going to tell you everything, Ruth.... Right now."

She sat there expressionless. The initial revelation was sinking in and she was bracing for fuller comprehension.

I've already started, as I promised.... I have to complete my story.

I told her the entire narrative. I told her about what I did in the war. I told her about my career in the SS in all its bloodstained pages. I told her about Rabbi Mordechai who read the Kaddish and the other rabbi who shook his fist in the air and others – many others. Some more memorable than others but all part of my infamous career. I told her that it didn't matter what my heart wanted to do, only what

I actually did. And that was too often nothing but helping with cold-blooded murder.

I told her about Plan O – my surgery, my escape, my new life.

"So, yes ... we've met. I've wished for many nights that I'd arrived sooner."

She listened to everything, her eyes fixed on mine, blinking only rarely. Late into the night, I finished.

Relief ... an unburdening of my soul. I'm ready for whatever lies in store.

She clutched my shirt and pulled me into the light.

"I remember his eyes distinctly. I felt her warm breath on my face as she nervously studied my features. Her eyes pierced painfully into mine, then into my soul. Her eyes became cold, analytic – no longer warm or at all friendly. They searched for the truth, brutal though it might be. Her face contorted as though in an ordeal.

Her short scream sent me reeling backward.

"Oh my God! It *is* you."

Her cry was of suppressed horror.

I didn't know what to do. I wanted to hold her, hug her and comfort her – but was I what I had been only a moment ago? I determined to let her make the decision. She opened her arms to me, but pulled them back with a gasp.

It took her so long to collect herself and all that she had believed in. She gently wiped her eyes and looked at me.

"I am sorry, Johann. I would like to go home now."

"Yes, of course ... I understand."

She gave me a parting glance, then left.

My arms remained opened, reaching towards her as she closed the door behind her.

A New Reality

I DID NOT SEE Ruth for well over a week and I was resigned to never seeing her again. One morning Anne came my door. I heard her footfalls stop several seconds before she could bring herself to knock. When I opened the door she looked at me nervously. She had been crying.

What has Ruth told her? Am I to be arrested?

"You need to see Ruth," she informed me with a look of sad desperation. "She was hospitalized last night."

My breathing stopped for a moment.

"You must see her. The doctors think her time is at hand."

I arrived at the Worcester hospital an hour later and soon was in Ruth's room on the fourth floor – a secluded room with large windows. It was the best room in the entire hospital, according to one of the nurses.

"It's for special patients," she told me.

Flowers had arrived from many members of the congregation and were arranged on the night table and windowsill and wherever a place could be found. I brought a Rose of Sharon plant from her garden.

Ruth was looking out the windows to take in the view of the quaint New England town and the rolling hills in the distance. A small copse was in view, its sparse foliage green and orange with autumn. Birds flew by and townspeople went cheerfully about with their lives. The sunshine gave them all a wonderful appearance, enhanced by the dire circumstances that strangely make us appreciate subtlety and beauty.

"All this will continue long after us," Ruth stated, acknowledging my presence.

"Yes ... all will go on without us."

"Please sit, Johann," she said, pointing towards an armchair near the window. "I have the most beautiful room in the entire hospital." Then she added mischievously, "See what connections can get you?"

Her sense of humor is still with us.

I sat down slowly and shared the view with her.

"So lovely...."

"I am sorry I left that night ... so very sorry."

"No, I am sorry ... for everything."

She took a deep breath and I noted a little difficulty in the task.

"I wanted you to know that I did not tell anyone – and I never will."

I looked downward.

"Thank you for telling me of your past, Johann. It made me understand your behavior towards me ... and towards us. It's not because you did not love me ... as I used to think for many months. And that's a great relief to me."

An affectionate smile came with her tears.

"I love you with all my heart, Ruth."

I raised my eyes towards hers.

"I always did ... and I always will."

"I know."

She nodded then wiped her eyes – as did I.

She bravely rose from her bed. I met her and pressed her to my heart.

"I do not have many days, Johann."

"Yes... I know."

"I have a request."

"Anything."

"Will you stay with me until the end?" Her eyes sparkled joyfully. "I want never to be apart from you."

"You've been with me always," I smiled. "And I'll never leave you."

And that's how it would be. They brought another bed into the finest room in the hospital – the one for the well connected only. I arranged for Ruth's favorite restaurant in Worcester to deliver food and we enjoyed our meals as ever. When Ruth felt up to it, we went to a garden on the hospital grounds, where despite the lateness in the year, lovely flowers were still to be found. Other times, we played cards and chatted. We talked about her life, good times and bad.

I told her about being born near Hamburg, about my childhood friends, about the first girl I had a crush on, and about my family – details that no one had heard since the war. When she asked about the war, I recounted events. Sometimes details about daily life and meals and bureaucratic things. Other times, about the more difficult matters.

After one painful revisiting of the latter sort, we both fell quiet.

"You carry too much, Johann," she told me.

I could not find words.

"I understand how you feel," she continued. "And I can understand why. The madness was more powerful than you. You couldn't have done more than you did without being killed yourself."

"Then perhaps I should have *been* killed."

"Perhaps," she responded softly, "but your need to survive pressed you ahead, into the system."

She touched my face.

"You were a survivor yourself, a simple survivor.... And you saved me."

"I could have saved ... more."

The last word came only with difficulty.

"At what price? You would have been killed yourself – and by your own people."

Ruth looked into my eyes, trying to add conviction to her words.

"Just desserts...." I said bitterly.

"Had you died at the hands of the SS, I would not have been saved and been able to go on to have such a wonderful life. We would never have met ... again.

"You wanted to save more people, you did not want to continue as a part of the system. But you had to. Military service in Germany had always been prided. It must have seemed part of every boy's destiny. Putting on the uniform entailed a great deal – living up to expectations and performing your duty. Otherwise … things would have fallen hard on you."

She saw I was not convinced.

"You know, Johann, there is a saying in the Talmud."

I raised my eyes to her and she continued.

"Whoever saves one life, saves the entire world."

She smiled gently as she pondered those words and the wisdom they hold.

"You saved me … and by putting fear into your officers and soldiers that day, many others were also saved. Summary executions went down in number.… You did well."

Those words from the Talmud were familiar somehow.

"I heard that saying before … but I can't remember just where."

Memory, over the years, becomes rather unreliable, and concerted effort to recall something can simply waste time – a commodity Ruth and I had little of. So I dropped the effort and had lunch sent up.

The next day was a bad one. Ruth was very weak. We stayed in her room all day as she mostly slept.

The following evening was a little better. She had some strength and wanted to see the garden again.

"But it's late and already dark. Are you sure, Ruth?"

"Yes, I'm quite sure."

"But.…"

A thought shot into my mind, but I did not dare explore it.

"Let's go see the beautiful night," I replied.

I covered her with a blanket and we went downstairs into an all but empty lobby.

"Be careful. It's a bit chilly tonight," cautioned the receptionist at the front desk.

"Thank you. It looks like a lovely night though," Ruth replied with a glowing smile.

"A young girl … probably in her early twenties. Her whole life is in front of her."

"Yes," I agreed as I held her arm and we went out into the garden. "She's just starting off."

"One soul at the end of its life, another at its outset. The young take it all for granted. Beautiful stars…. I am not taking anything for granted now. I want to enjoy this beautiful night."

She took a deep breath

"I love the fresh night air!" she declared with a laugh.

We sat on a stone bench amid a pair of small pine trees. The skies were clear and the street quiet. Only occasionally did a car or two glide by on its way to one place or another.

We held hands.

"Are you cold, Johann?"

She was concerned with me.

"Yes, a little."

"Here, let me hug you … and warm you."

She did both.

"You'll have to take care of yourself from now on, Johann. I will not be here to watch over you, you know."

I sadly nodded. I well knew that Ruth had made sure that I ate on time and dressed to the weather – a wife, almost.

Life becomes more beautiful when you've someone with you … someone who cares for you … someone who loves you. Life will not be the same. I'm not sure life….

"I am sorry I did not marry you," I said.

She held my face in her frail hands.

"I understand why. I understand you."

My voice broke.

"I am willing… we could – "

"Shhhh," she stopped me gently. "No need. I know that you love me."

She looked into my eyes. Her silver hair sparkled like shiny stars in the illuminated night.

"And you know I love you."

We kissed. The moon boldly proclaimed itself above us – an immense full moon.

I don't want this moment to end ... I do not want her to die.

If I could've gone on in her place, I'd have done so gladly. A pure soul.

A deep sadness fell over me. I buried my face deep into her shoulder and cried as I did when I was a child.

"I am sorry I left your house like that."

"No, you shouldn't be sorry," I protested. "You had every right to do so."

"I just needed time ... and then ... all this came up."

She looked down to her gaunt form.

"Hard news...."

"Still, had I not left, we could've had another beautiful week."

I had no words just then.

"I am going to leave you tonight, Johann."

Her time was at hand and there was nothing we could do to change it.

"It will not be forever, you know," she noted with a smile. "Only temporary. We will be together again ... later. I am sorry to wish for that but I feel that I already miss you...."

"I look forward to the day."

"You still have a reason to continue, you know. You have an important contribution in this world."

She knew what was going through my head.

"He is a wonderful little reason ... you mean so very much to him."

"Yes ... my friend Samuel."

"He needs you, Johann. They say that a child's judgment is never wrong. If a child sees you as a good person ... well then, you *are* a good person."

"Ah ... He's young still. Perhaps his judgment will improve!"

"You can't deny it. He loves you very much. That tells you everything."

"I'll see him tomorrow – I promise."

"It's good for him, it's good for you ... it's good for your soul."

We held each other as the hours passed and the streets became empty. Neither of us wanted to leave.

"Well, I am quite tired now."

Ruth looked at me with great love.

"Thank you, Johann, for giving me this beautiful final night. I am ready now."

I struggled with my emotions.

"Are *you* ready?" she asked.

I will never be ready, but it is not in our hands.

Gathering all my powers, I answered, "Yes."

"Then let's go to sleep … after this, the most beautiful night of my life."

I bravely held her arm as we reentered the hospital. A new nurse sat in the lobby, busy with paperwork.

Back in the finest room in the hospital, I helped her lie down then opened the curtains. The bright moon was there again for us.

"Ahhh, so lovely," Ruth murmured, truly astonished by the sight.

"Glorious."

"What a marvelous image to fall asleep … into."

"May I make a request, please? May I sleep with you this night?"

Ruth gingerly moved to make room.

We lay together transfixed by the large moon whose other-worldly light filled the room. I was reluctant to fall to sleep.

"I am tired now."

Ruth looked at my face at length, wanting to appreciate every detail, then lay her head upon my chest.

"This is the best way to go to sleep."

"Good night, Ruth. I love you with all my heart."

I kissed her.

"Good night, Johann. Wherever I go, I'll watch for you – the love of my life."

I caressed her silvery hair as her breathing slowed.

How can she know this is her last night? She will wake up in the morning, into another day.

Childish ideas of last-minute cures and heroic efforts passed though my mind, but sleep was overtaking me.

A cloud passed across the moon and I wanted to note it, but I let it be. The cloud must have continued its path, but I was asleep.

I woke up in the morning, alone. Two nurses, one black and the other Asian, stood near me, both in tears. I looked to my side and a strange but unmistakeable emptiness told me that Ruth was gone. The flowers near the bed bloomed with all their majesty and their sweet scent filled the room.

"With your permission, I'll take the Rose of Sharon," I told the nurses.

"Of course," one of them said. Both wiped tears quietly.

Ruth had gone out of my life and it would never be the same.

Life after Ruth

RUTH'S DEATH INTRODUCED A difficult, lonely time. It took me several months to return to life, and naturally Samuel was instrumental in that. I picked him up every day from school then spent afternoons with him, helping with homework and just having fun. If the weather permitted, we went for walks – often past Ruth's old house.

It was my house now; Ruth had bequeathed it to me. I kept it in good shape but did not really know what to do with it. I had enough money to last me – and comfortably too. Her house was more spacious than mine, but I rather liked my place. It was home. So Sam and I just went there to visit and maybe to reminisce a bit as well.

He was in first grade now and understood many things that other six-year-olds puzzled inconclusively over. I explained that Ruth was not with us anymore. She was in heaven, in the skies.

I decided to put Ruth's house in Samuel's name rather than in my own. It will be his when he grows up – a wonderful gift from her to him. While the full meaning of home ownership was beyond him, he was elated.

"It was very nice of Ruth," he told me one day. "When I go up to heaven, I'll thank her."

"That's a splendid idea, Sam. And very sweet too."

I wonder if I'll be able to see them there.

One day, after homework, he asked me to play war with him – something he had learned at school or on the television. At first we were both soldiers and we chased each other about the house and in the yard, shooting at each other with imaginary guns formed with our index fingers and thumbs. Then I had to be his prisoner. I don't really know where he got this idea but I complied. He chased me across the yard, over to a tall pine then onto the porch where I sat on a swing and humbly surrendered to my victorious foe.

"I got you!" he happily announced.

"Yes, I surrender, kind sir. You are so brave and bold. What you are going to do with me?" I asked feigning fear.

Unprepared for the question, he became perplexed.

"Don't know yet .... I know, I'll kill you!"

I felt sudden discomfort. I had seen this situation before. I tried to rid myself of the idea but could not. The memories hit me with all of their fury.

Parents had their children taken from them. Then their children were shot in front of them.

"But my friend, I have a child at home. If you kill me, he will not have a father anymore. Are you sure you want to do that?"

"Yes, I *have* to kill you."

He remained in his soldierly role.

"Samuel...." I spoke slowly this time. "If you kill me, the child at home will lose his father. He is waiting for me to come home. But if I die, I'll *never* come back home. My little boy will be very sad.... Are you sure this is what you want to do?"

His glee vanished and he lowered his hands, easing his finger-weapon. He looked at me wide-eyed – and in silence. The idea of losing a parent was beginning to frighten him.

"No, I will not kill you."

He smiled and his eyes flashed. My soul rejoiced!

"Thank you, Samuel. You did the right thing. It's not nice to kill anyone."

"Yes, you're right. The children at home will not have parents ... and they will be very sad."

The wisdom of a child.

"Yes, but not only because of that," I added as I put him on my lap. "We must never take human life. Every person wants to live. Even if they do not have children, they still want to live. This is the basic hope of every living thing on Earth."

"Yes...." He smiled and started to rock the swing. "We all want to live because we want to have fun. Maybe we also want to eat candy and go to the park."

"Exactly Samuel. You're a smart lad. Everyone wants to live and enjoy life. It's a basic right of nature."

We did not realize that then. So many did not recognize this basic right of human beings.

Where was my soul then?

Where was my country's soul?

I do not deserve to have his precious time. I do not deserve his love, his innocent love.

Samuel's voice took me out of my train of thoughts.

"I'll take you with me as my prisoner ... and we can play together!"

I laughed at the prosepct of playing with my noble captor.

"I wish that every soldier would do this to his prisoner! This is a very good thing, Samuel. You treat your prisoner nicely."

"That's what you would have done also, isn't it?"

I remembered something. I remembered when and where I heard, "Whoever saves one life, saves the entire world."

*   *   *

Winds that lashed down from the Baltic made Treblinka especially frigid in winter. As I drove out of the camp I heard shooting and screaming – more so than normal, that is. There was a work detail that was bringing in firewood from the adjacent forest. Soldiers were shooting prisoners at will, as though a lark. And for many, it was just that.

I tried to keep the killings down by insisting that arbitrary executions interfered with work schedules. But an SS regional commander overruled me. Not directly, of course. It was merely let out that my word was no longer above question and that I might be on the way out. There had been rumors, both at Treblinka and up the SS command structure, that I was becoming too weak to perform my duties and that I had received my posts through influence not performance. The former was true, the latter was not.

An inspection team came to Treblinka I in the late fall. There was something unusual about their demeanor towards me. They seemed to be looking into my eyes for something – a weakness, a flaw.

"Your schedules are always met, Herr Oberführer. Yet.... Do you question our program here ... or the ones at Treblinka II or Birkenau?"

Those places were of course death camps and their mention struck a nerve in me. I hoped I didn't flinch.

"Of course not," I replied with the crispness I knew they wanted. "It is an important undertaking that will benefit the Reich."

For the first time, I wasn't sure I believed this anymore.

"Does the sight of Jews being shot somehow offend you – in any way? If so, your abilities can be put to use elsewhere. We all know that men weary of this business and need to be transferred."

"Of course not," I repeated.

"It is essential that the men be able to use their own judgments in maintaining proper order – and in keeping up the spirits of the camp staff."

"Yes, that is so. Of course. Order and morale are essential to our efforts."

I'm sure my response was less than crisp that time. They looked at me intently for a while before saluting and heading for their Mercedes. On the way, they talked briefly with Schaffer and a senior sergeant. Schaffer turned and looked at me. He might have smiled but I can't be sure. A gust of wind struck and he turned away to shield his eyes.

The message was clear. I retained my position but my authority had been undermined. I requested transfer back to Germany or into a Waffen SS unit on one of the fronts, but the headquarter's answer was, "Not now ... with time. Your abilities in maintaining work schedules are singular and cannot be easily replaced."

One morning I took especial notice of the shooting of the prisoners on a firewood detail. Despite the new policy, my rage ignited and I drew my pistol and rushed to the scene, swearing to myself that if I saw any killings, I would shoot everyone involved. As I neared the scene, I saw soldiers aiming their Mausers at a boy. A half-dozen corpses were strewn about around him. He trembled as he awaited his fate.

"What is the meaning of this?" I asked with anger and authority.

A corporal jumped to attention, saluted and began his report.

"These prisoners tried to escape, Herr Oberführer."

"These men are nowhere near the fence … and they are rather close together," I noted pointedly, "hardly consistent with an escape attempt."

"Private Kuzmuk killed a prisoner – only then did the others try to escape."

He pointed towards one of his soldiers, who proudly brandished a Schmeisser machine pistol. He looked deranged to me. He saluted smartly then allowed a moronic look to cross his face.

"They are merely Jews, Herr Oberführer. We can kill them as we please."

"I did not give you permission to speak, idiot."

My shout brought unease to the soldiers.

"What is your name?" I asked the boy prisoner.

"Misha," he said quietly.

"What happened here, Misha?"

His Yiddish was marked with many Polish words but was readily understandable to most German speakers.

"We were working, hauling wood. Then a soldier started to shoot, without any reason. He killed my father."

He pointed to one of the corpses.

"Then he started to shoot the others. Only then did they try to run for the woods."

He's just a child.

I closed my eyes as he continued.

"I did not run. I knew that would mean death … so I remained."

He raised his eyes to mine and asked, "Are you going to kill me?"

I cannot show weakness here, not in front of the soldiers.

"You soldiers! Back to the camp and come back with more

prisoners for the work detail. We need wood for heating. Private Kuzmuk! You will remain."

Kuzmuk was clearly dismayed.

Misha was afraid; he stood with his face down.

Neither of them knew what to expect.

I took away Kuzmuk's machine pistol, made sure the safety was on then smashed it across his face, breaking his jaw, I'm sure. He fell unconscious to the ground. The boy remained in his spot, trembling – maybe even more so than before.

"Misha, I am very sorry your father died," I told him quietly.

He did not answer. He was almost certainly dumbfounded by such behavior from an SS officer. To our right, just outside the rows of barbed wire, there were thick woods – a dense forest that Jews at camps all over Poland dreamed of escaping into. The gate was still open.

"Run, Misha. Run into the woods," I urged him.

"You will not shoot me in the back?" he asked fearfully.

He knew all too well that telling inmates to flee then shooting them was a favorite sport of the guards.

"No, I will not. This, I swear. You have a chance out there. I swear to you I will not shoot you."

He looked at Kuzmuk's unconscious form and judged me if not trustworthy, then at least quite different. With a trembling voice, I all but pleaded with him.

"Look Misha, I do not know how this madness came upon us. I wish I could stop it, but I can't – I simply can't. I am only one man."

I stopped my confession for a second, making sure it was not too much for the boy. He just stared at me in disbelief.

"I wish to survive, as do you. Yes, I am on the other side ... but I feel the same.... It kills me inside. I wish I could do more. I wish I could save more.... It kills me inside."

Misha was still incredulous, but he was able to speak.

"We are religious – observant. My father and I say every morning and evening our prayers."

I saw gathering strength in his eyes.

"We have a saying, 'Whoever saves one life, saves the entire world.' "

My eyes filled with tears and I quickly wiped them.

"Every one you save, you save an entire world."

I wanted to hug him, but the fear of being seen was overwhelming. Moments of compassion, in war and in madness, must remain fleeting.

Kuzmuk started to groan and move. A boot to his temple put him back into his previous state.

"You are a good man," Misha told me. "I can see that."

"Yes, well.... I am the commander here, aren't I," I said bitterly. "You have to run, Misha – quickly. I'll close the gate behind you. You have a chance out there. Go north. There are partisans there."

Misha looked at me, then at the gate, then again at me.

"Thank you...."

He started to run, but stopped and looked back.

"I'll never forget you," he said then raced off.

"Good luck, little one," I said to myself.

It looked as though his feet never touched the ground.

Run ... run like hell ... out of here.... He'll be far away before the next headcount.

I smiled as he disappeared into the forest outside Treblinka. I walked to the gate and closed it.

Later on I was brought to a military board – a sort of court martial – where I stood accused of assaulting Kuzmuk. I declared that he disobeyed orders; the other soldiers asserted that I hit him without reason. The court decided that I had been under enormous stress and that I should be moved to a different camp.

The next camp was no better at all. I was transferred to Monowitz, an immense labor camp two hundred miles to the southwest, where I would perform administrative duties only.

Misha's absence was not noted at later head counts. With so many arbitrary killings, it was hard to keep track. To this day I wonder what happened to him.

*   *   *

"Johann, is that what you'd do?" Samuel repeated his question to me.

"Yes, of course, Samuel. I would do the same. I would treat my prisoners well."

We continued playing and chatting until Anne arrived.

"Did you guys have fun today?" She asked merrily.

"Yes, mom. We played soldiers and prisoners. It isn't nice to kill prisoners, mom," Samuel explained seriously.

"Of course, Samuel."

Anne gave me a quizzical look.

"Nothing ... just a game," I said dismissively. "Something he probably learned from kids in school or on TV. Enjoy your evening, Anne."

Later that night I sat on my rocking chair and looked to the heavens, remembering my conversations with Ruth. I spoke aloud.

"Ruth ... I remember where I had heard that saying. It was back then ... with a religious child named Misha. I could not save his father ... but I hope I saved him."

I thought about those words for a while. Ruth and Misha were right. Any saved soul is a world by itself. I wish I could have saved more. I wish I had never been involved with the war. But I could not change that. I was born into a social reality and lived within it. No justification, though. I should have found a way to tell the world about the madness. I should have at least run away from everything.

I needed her, I needed Ruth. I needed her presence, her essence – to hold at night. I needed her soul with mine. Only her vibrant memory remained with me.

"I miss you," I said into the night – not even a moon to answer me. Lonely stars sparkled here and there in the inky darkness. The universe looked bleak and empty.

There was an especially bright star off in the eastern sky.

Is it my imagination or is this star becoming brighter by the second?

Indeed in a far corner of the sky an audacious star seemed to grow in intensity and move towards me.

"Is it you, Ruth?" I called out. "Is it you?"

The star halted its growing magnitude but remained fixed there for hours. I had no doubt what it was.

It is Ruth.

She is here to encourage me and to help me through these hard times.

I love you, Ruth.

She remained there until I drowsed in my armchair. For hours, my soul would not let me sleep. I did not want to leave my magnificent star. Near dawn, I did fell asleep. I woke up soon thereafter, without her. The sun of the new day had overwhelmed the stars in the firmament.

"Good morning, Ruth."

I decided to write my memoirs – to elaborate my confessions, explore my thoughts and hopefully bring closure to my torment. I wrote down everything. I wrote about an ambitious youth eager for the glory and fame that the military promised. I followed my ambition and indeed became an officer in the German military. Fate played a cruel joke on me and put me in the military during the Third Reich. I rose through the ranks throughout those years and during World War Two as well.

I came to see that militaries all too often act against humanity and basic laws as well, but my desire to succeed pressed me forward – and upward. My inner-self asserted its presence from time to time and told me that all this was wrong, very wrong. But my practical side prevailed, saying it's war. War brings out the worst in us, including acquiescence and complicity.

After the war, when fuller information came to us and time granted us better perspective, I had the time to reflect upon those days. The world around me made me look back on the one behind me and see its horror and evil.

Chance, or fate, brought into my life a wonderful boy – a wonderful Jewish boy. He showed me his goodness and the goodness within me, which for all its welcomeness also showed me, in bold contrast, my sinister side. One side is bright and shiny, the other dark and malevolent. The darkness, I know, will always be with me. The healing powers of time are not limitless. My past will stay with me until my final day.

My final day would long ago have come had it not been for Samuel. And if today were that day, Samuel would grieve tremendously. I have to go on until he is older, when he can accept the death of a loved one. Fate has me yearning to live for the sake of a Jewish lad.

Maybe Ruth was right. Maybe saving a few souls during the war earned me the gift of Samuel's unconditional love. The idea has some appeal to my ego but only a little resonance in my heart.

A greater power is in control of these matters. This greater power holds sway in all things, determining the past, present and future. It is far greater than I am. I submit myself to its will, and one day to its judgment as well.

One day someone will read this. Perhaps many will.

One morning there came a knock on my door.

"Come in," I called out.

I am not expecting anyone.

"Good morning, Johann!" Rabbi Levi stepped in with a buoyant look. "I am sorry to interrupt your morning."

"Not at all." I greeted him with genuine warmth. "You are always welcome at my house. Please do come in. May I offer you something?"

"Thank you, a glass of water will be just the thing," he replied as he took off his fedora and sat. "What a gorgeous morning!"

"Indeed. I love fall mornings. They are not too hot, not too cold. Perfect warmth for aging people like us."

"I absolutely agree. These are also my favorite mornings. Summer is too hot and winter I do not need to tell you ... freezing. Fall and spring are temperate – a golden mean." He chuckled and added, "Wouldn't it be wonderful if the entire world were in a golden mean? No extremes, no disagreements ... everyone compromising for the other. Peace ... no war."

"A great world, but an imaginary one," I offered back. "It will never happen. The human race is too possessive, selfish and does not think about consequences."

Rabbi Levi bobbed his head about as he collected his thoughts, then pointed to the horizon.

"Just imagine how many wars would be prevented. A world without war, crime or hate. Imaginary? Yes, but still something worth hoping for!"

"Yes...." I released a long sigh. "That's something that would change many things in life, but this is an academic discussion and I am ... a Swiss businessman."

We both sank into our thoughts – quite different ones, I thought.

"Well ... anyway. I came to visit to tell you how sorry I was to hear about Ruth. She was an amazing woman. I met her only once or twice but clearly she was a great woman.... I am truly sorry for you and for all who knew her."

"Thank you. She was a special person. And I loved her." I straightened my look into the rabbi's eyes. "I loved her with all my heart."

He fell quiet.

"Excuse me for intruding upon your private life, but I'd like to know ... why didn't you marry her?"

His scrutiny displayed both puzzlement and concern. It was my turn to look to the horizon.

"I don't really know, Rabbi Levi...."

My answer was hardly an answer. We both knew that. He became silent once more but then continued.

"I came to visit her one day ... in the hospital. You were not there yet. We had a talk.... I knew that you both loved each other – Anne told me that and I could see it in both of you when you sat together in the synagogue."

He paused for a sip of water.

"I asked her why you two didn't marry and she said she couldn't tell me. She didn't say she *didn't* know. She said she *couldn't* say – and that's quite another thing. I was curious – or concerned – and tried to coax her ... but I was unsuccessful."

Now he looked deeply into me.

"She said that only *you* could tell me."

Yes, she kept our secret.

"Why, Johann? What can stop a person from marrying his love?"

"It's difficult, Rabbi Levi," I answered curtly.

" Of course it's difficult. Important things are always difficult. You know I am your friend … you can tell me anything. I'll keep it confidential. No one will ever know.… It will also be better for you. You'll unburden your heart."

He honestly wants to help me.

"I feel you have a great pain inside you. You have to get it out. It looks to me that you shared it with Ruth – and this is good … progress … moving ahead. I am sure it brought her closure.… I would like to know also. I would like to help you, Johann. But you have to help me help you."

Such honesty in his eyes.

"Thank you. Maybe one day."

I smiled faintly – an attempt to end this line of questioning.

"Is it your health?"

I shook my head.

"Something in your past? An error … bad judgment … perhaps a crime?"

The last word elicited an immediate verbal reply this time.

"Yes, it is something in my past … many years ago."

My voice was elevated. I released a long, calming sigh.

"I am sure that there is an explanation for whatever it is that you've done, Johann. Even for the worst offenses there are reasons and explanations. You do not look to me to be a bad person. I cannot imagine something too bad that you could have committed."

I looked at his face without saying a word. He had the face of a pleasant person, long and narrow, accented with a graying beard – the pride of his calling. That pride was shared by his peers in Europe – and elsewhere, I imagine. Back through the centuries, too. He looked like many of the rabbis in those days – gray or graying beards and kindness in their eyes. Noble figures, out of the ordinary, full of goodness and willing to give.

And willing to forgive as well.

*   *   *

He knew that we were going to kill him, yet I never saw hatred in his eyes. Quite the contrary, I saw almost love and compassion towards the world in general – and most strikingly, toward my men and me. That was something I could never understand. A rabbi about to be killed has compassion for me, compassion for my soldiers. Why? There must be something astonishing in a man who has taken this path.

*   *   *

I looked again at Rabbi Levi. Physical things such as wrinkles and bushy eyebrows stood out in that profound moment, but said nothing. The arresting thing was his eyes. The bright, decent essence behind his blue eyes, which announced that his entire being wanted to help – to help even me, a former SS officer.

He deserves to know … come what may.

Another Confession

"**Y**OUR INSTINCTS ARE RIGHT, Rabbi Levi," I began blankly, "I've done terrible things."

I looked for a response but there was none. He only awaited the unfolding of my story.

"More terrible than you can imagine ... I hope...." I added the last two words upon a moment's reflection.

"I was an SS officer."

I paused then continued.

"I served the Third Reich. I commanded a work camp at Treblinka ... and later, one at Monowitz. I had a part in the Final Solution."

He continued looking at me, expressionless.

Did he already know that ... or does he conceal his reactions well?

"Are you ready to hear my entire story?" I asked.

Rabbi Menachem Levi nodded slowly and leaned forward intently, perhaps also bracing himself.

I began with my childhood and my attraction to National Socialism and my rise in the SS. I described some of the actions we conducted in Polish villages.

Still, he showed no reaction.

He is too angry ... or too incredulous.... His eyes still convey compassion....

I told the story of the rabbi who wanted to say Kaddish for his students and community, just before we killed him. That account – the one mostly harshly seared into my memory – elicited the rabbi's first discernible response. His eyes opened wide, as though in controlled astonishment. Nonetheless, he only shook his head slightly and whispered, "Yes, I understand ... I understand...." He ran his fingers through his beard, unconsciously.

I gave my account of Ruth that day in Treblinka – Schaffer ... the baby Sara ... running towards them.

A monster ... I'm sure he will call me that.

How many other horrific stories had he heard – from countless victims whose lives had been devastated all across the continent of Europe, from France and Holland to the steppes of Russia – wherever the black uniforms of the SS had been. An emotional response must be churning within him and in a moment it will erupt from him, from his soul, from his accumulated moral reasonings.

He will condemn me....

The lightning had flashed and I awaited the thunder.

"Johann ... you saved a human life ... you saved Ruth's life...." he whispered with awe and astonishment.

I trust this man.

"Yes, but I did not save her baby," I added bitterly.

"That is why you couldn't marry her – you carried this burden, this guilt?"

"Yes," I answered in obvious anguish. "I could never get that out of me ... and away from us. I wanted to protect her and to give her anything she wanted in order to compensate for what I'd done and not done."

"But all she really wanted was you."

He completed a thought that was forming in my mind.

I nodded.

"And you could not give yourself to her because of what happened that day."

Again, I nodded.

"Well, you two were together ... all the way to the end. Anne told me."

"Yes, and I am glad I was there for her," my eyes filled with tears and I wiped them slowly. "We went to sleep together on her last night. I woke up alone … but I held her as she passed from this world.… She did not die alone."

"This is a remarkable story, Johann. Truly remarkable. There are many troublesome things, but remember that you saved her many years ago. A higher power brought you two back together, and you were with her during her last moments with us."

Rabbi Levi was fascinated.

I was with my memories of Ruth; Rabbi Levi thought through my account.

I broke the silence by finishing the story of my escape and arrival in Massachusetts.

"Your plan brought you here."

He looked amazed.

"Yes, I am a new person. I have a new face, a new identity. No one from my past can recognize me."

"Why did you visit the country of Israel?"

Rabbi Levi looked puzzled.

I looked out into space to gather my thoughts on this.

"Initially, I was reluctant … afraid. Ruth was the one who wanted to go. But my views having changed so much since the war, I was curious about the country. I had read about Israel since its establishment and even come to admire its people. I also read about Yad Va Shem … I wanted to see it."

Rabbi Levi's eyes prompted me to continue.

"And I saw it. I saw all the things that we did. I faced the unimaginable, the inhuman. It was very painful. The enormity of our actions hit me with all its might, with all its powers. Furthermore, we met there a woman – herself a survivor. She told her story of escape. Heartbreaking … unforgettable."

I needed a break – only a momentary one. But I needed to go on.

"May I offer you more water, Rabbi Levi?"

"Yes, please. How thoughtful."

He smiled pleasantly as I brought his water, though he was deep in thought.

"You know," I continued, "every person in this world wants to know his contribution to the world."

I laughed dryly and cynically.

"My contribution … with an occasional matter here and there … has not been for the good. I grew up wanting to do good – to save people – but…."

My pause was calculated to invoke a response from Rabbi Levi, but he did not speak.

What can you say to a person responsible for many horrors. Nothing, simply nothing.

"I am ready to face the consequences," I continued without a blink. "I am not a young person anymore but this is without any relation to my age. If the authorities show themselves tomorrow at my doorstep and put me into a trial, I will face any punishment without complaint.

"If I were the judge at my trial, I would give the death sentence – exactly as happened at Nuremberg, exactly as happened with Eichmann. Everyone should get his punishment according to the law. The people must show the world and the next generations that actions like these must never happen again. Not with Jews, not with blacks and not with any other race or nation."

Rabbi Levi nodded silently. A flurry of emotions passed across his face. He looked perplexed. I certainly was.

"Thank you, Johann, for telling me all this. Your secret remains safe with me. You have my word on that. Further, if there is anything I can help you with, I will gladly help."

He released a long sigh and sat back on the chair.

"I've heard many extraordinary stories in the course of my rabbinical work and in life in general. I've met thieves and adulterers and even a murderer. Your story without doubt is the most difficult one."

He paused.

"I'll tell you my thoughts. The most important thing is that you realize what you have done and that you deeply regret your actions. I see the enormous burden on your soul and I see that you are tormented every moment by what you've done…."

"But Johann, despite your upbringing and training that led you there, your soul resisted it and rebelled against it. Had you intervened more forcefully than you did, you would have been killed yourself. Our will to continue living is strong. That is part of what makes us human. That is why we are fallible.

"You helped people, Johann. You saved Ruth, you saved that boy Misha. Do not dwell on what you did *not* do; think of what you *did* do. *Whoever saves one life, saves the entire world.* There is great wisdom in those words."

I responded immediately.

"Yes, I understand, but for so many years I accepted the ideals of National Socialism. Ambition led me to accept what was going on to get promoted – and promoted I was. That was wrong, very wrong. How many died on my watch? How many babies were buried alive? How many old people starved? I commanded part of that machinery of death."

"But were you really in command?" he shot back.

"If you had given the order to stop it all and to dismantle the camp, would the inmates have been sent home to live out their days?"

I moved about uneasily in my armchair.

"Then I should have quit the military and moved away. I should have gotten away from it. I could easily have slipped across the border into Switzerland."

"Perhaps, but would Ruth have been saved? What about Misha?"

"But many others would not have been killed!"

"Those would have killed with or without you."

I ran out of words. There was merit in his arguments, but the feeling of responsibility would not leave me. I was involved in those crimes and I had not yet atoned for them.

Rabbi Levi put his hand on my back.

"You have changed, Johann. Just think about it. When you came here, you hated Jews. You learned from your new neighbors – got to know them. You became part of the Rosenberg family – and became Samuel's *sandak*. You came to see the humanity in people whose humanity you denied. How many reports are there of Nazi criminals who have kept their hatred of Jews. They lurk in Paraguay and Brazil and such places – and regret nothing. These men would boast of their murderous deeds today were it not for the danger it would place them in. Not you, Johann ... not you."

He smiled encouragingly.

"But I have great pain, Rabbi Levi."

I held my head in my hands.

"I cannot stop seeing those murdered under my command – thousands of them. I cannot get rid of the feeling of responsibility – that I was there, on the wrong side."

A silence suggested the rabbi knew he could not dispel all my guilt that day.

"Johann, I would like to visit you more often – if it's not a burden on you, of course."

"Yes, please. I am here every morning. In the afternoon I am watching Samuel and...."

"Yes, I understand.... You two are lucky to have each other. Anne told me how much he loves you.... A child's innocent love is not given to bad people.... And such love is priceless."

He began to leave but needed to add something.

"There is an old Hasidic saying, 'A man must descend very low to find the force to rise again.'

We must search for this force for you."

He touched the brim of his fedora and with that, he was off.

I remained with my conflicting thoughts.

Will he expose me? I could of course deny everything. After all my documentation.... No ... I'll admit everything and face trial ... and Eichmann's fate. I'll tell the court everything of my upbringing and career. The court will judge me and determine my fate – according to law, not decree or whim or hatred.

To escape my confusion I looked outside into the beautiful forest beyond my fence. The tall trees proclaimed their majesty in magnificent greens amid a splendid day – a day to live for.

Rabbi Levi kept his word. He did not expose me but instead visited me once a week. I opened up more to him. Before there were therapists, there were rabbis. He listened raptly, with only an occasional comment.

"If you judge people, you can't love them," he once said.

Sometimes we had breakfast together and even went for walks. Rabbi Levi was an interesting fellow. I learned that a rabbi is a person who has achieved a level of learning, in one field or another, after many years of study. A rabbi must be a leader and must be an inspiration to his community. Some rabbis are dispatched to faraway places in order to provide for the Diaspora.

The rabbi and his family create and maintain a community – a *kehila* – which includes the synagogue, school, daycare and giving members of the *kehila* any help they can offer. The calling requires helping not only Jews but any person who asks for it. Rabbi Levi once mentioned that prisoners, Jewish and gentile, had asked to see him. He of course complied.

"My job is to visit the person, in jail or in a hospital or any other place, and listen to his words, sometimes his last words. I impart to them the Bible's wisdom, its ways. In so doing, I try to bring them peace. I look for the light in a person's heart. It matters not what the person did in life – it is not ours to decide."

Such devotion and faith.

"People see with their eyes, God sees the souls. If your soul has good, it will be seen by the greater power."

His wisdom and warmth encouraged me.

"The Bible can have mercy but it can also be blunt – and merciless when needed. Evil people were executed and criminals punished, then and today."

I liked his honesty and integrity.

"Johann, I would like to ask you to think about coming to the synagogue for next Thursday night's service," he asked one morning over breakfast.

"Is there anything special that night?" I asked in between bites of a salt bagel.

"Yes, it's Holocaust Remembrance Day. It is a special day in Israel and we observe it here in America."

An old fear reminded me that it was still there.

"If you are not comfortable, I can understand. But if you do want to come, I'd love to have you take part."

He looked for my reaction.

"What will the service include? Is there a special ceremony?"

"No, we are conducting our regular evening prayer but adding the Kaddish for all the Jews who were killed during the Holocaust."

"I noticed that people say it for deceased relatives. As you will remember, I once heard a rabbi saying a Kaddish."

"The Kaddish," Rabbi Levi explained, "is praise and sanctification of God's name. Various versions of the Kaddish are used but the term usually means the prayer in our mourning ritual. It graces all our prayer services and funerals and memorials. A person says the Kaddish on the passing of relatives or for any loved one who has gone on. This Thursday we are saying a Kaddish for all the Holocaust's many victims."

I can still hear the Polish rabbi's voice in my head. I can still see his face, wrapped with his striped cloth, moving back and forth in his prayer.

"Yes, I would very much like to attend the service," I said.

I wanted to be there.

My Kaddish

WHEN I ARRIVED, THE chamber was alive with dozens of gathered voices. I looked about at the artwork as usual then headed for my seat far in the back. I had come to take in the ambience of the synagogue. I loved the energy. Purity and goodness were everywhere. Rabbi Levi radiated it and the people and artifacts returned it. I enjoyed being there, though only as an outsider.

Rabbi Levi excused himself from a group of people and came over to me.

"Good evening, Johann. So glad to see you here tonight. I reserved you a seat – in the front. Please...."

I liked to be alone with my thoughts and not immersed in the service. I seldom paid attention to the rite. I preferred to meditate – my time with the higher power. But tonight would be different. Rabbi Levi led me to a seat in the front row and introduced me to a group there.

"This is Johann – one of our newest members."

"Nice to meet you. My name is Robert and this is Henry."

We all shook hands – quite warmly, I thought.

"My pleasure," I answered as I took my seat.

"So sorry to hear about Ruth," Robert added.

"Thank you. So kind of you."

I looked around and saw members of the congregation sharing experiences and common concerns. There was a true community there in that synagogue, something that was disappearing in much of modern America. Soon enough the rabbi asked for silence and the service started.

That night I found myself following the prayers and rituals. Those about me looked in their prayer books, knew when to stand, when to join the prayers and when to listen. The Torah case was beautifully appointed. I knew by then that the Torah is stored in the case and taken out at prescribed moments in the services. It seemed to hold within it ... oh, I don't know ... heritage, wisdom, hope.

"Members of the congregation," Rabbi Levi began in a serious voice, "today, as we all know, is a special day, a day of remembrance and mourning for our brothers and sisters who were murdered in the madness that was Nazism."

I concentrated on his words as they reverberated in the wood-paneled chamber.

"During the early morning, local time here, a siren was heard across the state of Israel, beginning a day of mourning and remembrance – Holocaust Remembrance Day."

He paused and looked out upon the rapt audience.

"Holocaust Remembrance Day is a time for us Jews all around the world to remember. It is a day that we mourn the Jews and non-Jews that were brutally and mercilessly killed by the Nazis. For many of us it means personal sadness. Many of us are personally connected to this tragic period of history. Many of us had relatives who died in the Holocaust.

"On this day I would like to say a special Kaddish. In addition to the traditional Kaddish that each person says for close relatives, I would like to say this special Kaddish for the six million of our people murdered in the Holocaust."

Something moved inside me, demanding to be released. I felt a need to tell the people gathered there who I am and what I did. I wanted to tell these people who had personally felt the brutal hand of the Third Reich. Most will hate me. Many will wish to turn me in. Some may wish to attack me. But I felt ready ... ready to be judged. My mind raced about, doubting my decision, doubting my judgment – doubting my very sanity.

I am ready to be judged.

Rabbi Levi completed his preface and was about to start the Kaddish prayer, when I stood up.

"With your permission, Rabbi Levi, I would like to speak to the congregation."

I slowly turned around and faced them. All eyes turned to me. The rabbi looked at me with concern. My soul felt elevated, ennobled – uplifted by the prospect of unburdening it.

"My name is Johann Kraus and I live in Webster. Maybe a few of you have seen me here, as I am an occasional visitor to your town and its synagogue."

Rabbi Levi had a look of consternation as he wondered where my speech was going.

"I am not Jewish, yet I enjoy coming to your house of worship, perhaps especially today on Holocaust Remembrance Day. I need to tell my story to you all. It is not a pleasant story. It is a personal story, *my* personal story."

Many looked on intently, all but sure I was going to give an account of a harrowing escape from a camp somewhere in Poland or Germany. Rabbi Levi knew different and he motioned for me to confer with him. I approached him on the marble dais.

"Johann, what are you doing? What are you doing?" he whispered.

I felt a peaceful, world-weary smile come to me.

"It's time."

"Time for what?"

"Time to unburden my soul," I answered quietly. "This day ... this commemorative day ... is the best time I can think of. Your kind permission to continue?"

He was incredulous and becoming emotional.

"Johann, you ... I don't know how this will be taken. It could lead to ... you might not.... I did not ask you here for this."

"I am sure this is what I must do."

I shook his hand to ease his concern and fortify myself as well. He calmed and acquiesced.

"I will be ready to step in," he whispered.

I turned to the congregation, which was looking about trying to comprehend what was going on right in front of them. Some still expected an edifying escape story; others sensed that something was wrong. I had never felt so sure of the honorable nature of any action of mine.

"All of you have heard tragic stories about the Holocaust told in gripping often agonizing detail. My story is quite different. My story is from the other side, from the side of the SS ... and the Third Reich."

Murmurs ran through the congregation.

"Some parts will sound made-up, even absurd, but I assure you that every word is true – though I wish it were not the case. I ask but one thing – that you please let me finish my story. I want to relate my story to its end ... here tonight."

Rabbi Levi spoke up.

"Yes, I too request that his story be heard by all ... the entire story. Let none of us denounce him or judge him until his story is heard in full."

Looks of puzzlement and interest were everywhere in the silent room, but the rabbi's words had their effect. I took a deep breath and wondered of my own words' effect.

"My name is Johann Kraus ... but this is not my real name. I was born in Germany in the year 1910. I joined the Nazi Party in 1932 and eight years later I entered the German military – not the Wehrmacht, the SS. I started as a private but very quickly became an officer."

Whispers and gasps were heard. Some thought I was insane or making a cruel joke on a sacred night. When the commotion subsided, I continued.

"I became the commander of the Treblinka work camp in December of 1942."

I looked over to Rabbi Levi. He was blotting sweat from his brow. He looked out at the people and then at me. He seemed proud that his congregation was respectful of my and his wish. Maybe some were curious but I think most were in shock. After all, there before them stood an agent of the Final Solution.

Once I began, I felt something pushing me onward, to go on with my brutal narrative, confessing my complicity. I felt at home with myself, at peace with myself. Whatever would befall me ... well, that was not in my hands. I may be jeered, I may be attacked, I may be handed over to a tribunal somewhere in the world. It was all the same to me. My soul was at peace.

Two long hours. It took two long hours to complete my story. Thankfully, the rabbi brought me a glass of water about halfway through, and I thanked him for that. True to their esteemed rabbi's wish, the congregation let me tell my story in all its dreadful entirety.

"What we did was an unspeakable crime against humanity. History has spoken in one voice on that. And here I am, standing in front of you, taking full responsibility for my actions. I am aware that you may seek legal action or retribution in one way or another. I am aware that I may face trial – and even the hangman's noose. I accept this....

"As much as I would like to, I cannot ask your forgiveness. An enormity of such a scale cannot be adequately judged by man. Yes, they can sentence me to prison or to death but the forgiveness I seek can only come from a greater power ... a higher court. I am not sure that I will be forgiven ... not sure at all."

I looked into the congregation. Upon the various faces there I could see disbelief, anxiety, fear, and here and there even a little compassion. There must have been some anger and disgust, but I did not see it. I saw Elliott and Anne in their places but could not read any reaction on their faces.

The sound of someone clearing his throat came from the back and a man in his fifties stood and walked to the front with the help of a cane. He stared right at me as he approached and I expected the worst. As he reached the front he cleared his throat once more and spoke in a surprisingly strong voice.

"You saved Ruth.... Always remember that. You saved Ruth. I am new to Worcester and this synagogue but I've heard of this wonderful woman. You … saved … Ruth," he repeated, enunciating each word distinctly. "I was not lucky enough to meet Ruth, as you were."

"Yes … I loved her."

"You do not even know.… She was devastated back then … back in the work camp. She lost her husband and child. She lost her will to live – until I brought her my little brother."

The rabbi offered the elderly gentleman a chair. He sat, breathed in and continued.

"My little brother Alex was a shy young child then. We had lost our parents in the camp –both shot to death. He was just a six-year-old then. Alex was terribly affected. He could hardly sleep, cried most of the time and fell into a deep depression. I'm sure he would have died soon – I'd seen it too many times in the camps. The night I brought Alex to Ruth – over in her barracks – her motherly instincts immediately saw a child in need, though she herself was mired in depression as well.

"She took care of him and coaxed him out of his gloom. Because of her, because of her compassion, he survived. One day Alex and a handful of others escaped. At the time, I was too weak to run, so our ways parted. He escaped into the forest and after the war and the DP camps, eventually made it to the land of Israel. He lives there to this day."

He gave me a toothy smile that warmed my heart in a way that few others ever have.

"I am very glad to hear that story. Ruth made no mention of Alex."

"She nurtured him, she found him food, and she gave him love. She gave him the will to live – and that is why he survived. I have no doubt of that."

He looked at me through his thick glasses, impressing upon me his belief.

"You saved Ruth, she saved Alex. He survived, went to Israel and had a family of his own.… So you saved many people by saving just one. And I would like to thank you for that … here, on this special night."

Whoever saves one life, saves the entire world.

I hugged the old man and patted him on the back as he returned to his seat in the back, still uttering repeatedly, "He saved Ruth... He saved Ruth...."

The rabbi's voice came louder and more passionate than usual.

"I heard Johann's story not long ago. Yes, he served in the SS. Yes, under his command brutal crimes were committed. But could he have stopped these hideous actions? After lengthy thought, my conclusion is that *he could not.*"

His voice positively boomed with the last words. As the reverberation eased, he walked from side to side and continued.

"What I see is a young man thrown into a horrible reality. Yes, there were many human monsters then – no doubt. But I am sure there were many men like Johann and many incidents that have not yet been told. Maybe they died, maybe they were ashamed, or maybe they feared retribution...."

Rabbi Levi approached me and put his hand on my shoulder.

"This man ... Johann Kraus ... saved Jews. And we a have witness – our friend in the back there – as to the many joyous results of that. There was Alex and his family in Israel."

My eyes remained cast down to the marble floor.

"Surrounded by cruelty and brutality, he nonetheless tried to do his best to save Jews. Unfortunately, he could not save everyone. He could not save as many as he wanted. Had he overreached ... he would have been killed himself."

Rabbi Levi then hugged me – there, in front of his congregation. I thought it was the bravest and most human thing I ever witnessed.

"When I invited Johann to join us tonight, I did not imagine that he would confess his past to us. It was his choice entirely. As Johann lived his life in America he began to see the evil done by the Third Reich. Through his neighbors and their precious son, he learned to see the humanity in all of us. That is why Johann is ready to face the consequences. He attaches only passing significance to his acts of courage in saving people. I do not. I find his acts courageous ... and I am both grateful and in awe. He knows – as do we – that true forgiveness cannot come from us humans, but only from a greater power. We see only with our eyes, the greater power than us sees into souls."

When Rabbi Levi concluded, I expected a reaction – or numerous conflicting reactions – from the people, but there was only silence. I cannot say what everyone was thinking in that silence. I only know that I was in awe of the man.

Rabbi Levi returned us to the evening's purpose.

"I would like to continue with the Kaddish prayer for the six million Jews that were murdered in the Holocaust. May they all rest in peace."

He opened his prayer book.

"With your permission," I found myself talking again to the entire congregation, "I would like to participate in this prayer. Though I have been here several times, I've never participated in any of your prayers. But with your permission, I would like to participate in the Kaddish ... for the memory of all the people murdered in the Holocaust."

The silence was unsettling to me.

"Is there any objection to Johann's request?" Rabbi Levi asked.

"I do not know the Hebrew, but I would like to read the English version."

More silence.

"I'll help you, Johann," someone next to me said. "We will both say the prayer. I'll show you the English words."

With a shaky voice I added, "I would like to say this prayer for all the children, elderly, women and men, that I could not save. I am very sorry I could not save them all."

Tears rose in my eyes and my voice cracked.

"I only wish that I could have died instead of them."

The congregation began to recite the Kaddish as the fellow next to me pointed to the English words. Each word had a special meaning to me. Each word passed through my heart and soul. It was a prayer that seemed to come from inside me. It was my request for forgiveness from all whom I could not save. It was a prayer for all those who were murdered in the Holocaust.

At the end of the prayer my soul felt better. I had told the truth, at last. I did not feel any forgiveness, but I did not truly expect any. I only wanted the world to know who I was and that I was remorseful.

I slept well that night – better than I had in a long time.

Savior

MY GREATEST CONCERN WAS that Elliot and Anne would take Samuel out of my life. Samuel, like most of the younger children, was not present for the solemn commemoration that night. When I told my story I did not mention Anne or Elliot's names as among those I had met and learned from. I did not want to implicate them in any way. Most of all, I did not want to hurt Samuel.

To my relief Anne brought him the next day. It was spring vacation and Samuel was going to be with me for the whole week. It was cold but sunny – the kind of day we enjoyed outdoors before the heat and humidity of summer came.

"Good morning, Anne," I said quite tentatively.

"Good morning Johann. How are you today?" she replied matter-of-factly.

Her warm smile assured me.

Samuel ran to me and gave me a bear hug. Anne approached me and gently took my hand.

"That was a remarkable story. Shocking of course, but at the same time truly remarkable – and moving."

Her eyes were agog with interest.

"You underwent quite an ordeal to reach your new life."

I nodded.

"That was Plan O – the "O" symbolizing a trap surrounding me. When the world closed on Nazi Germany, we activated the plan."

Anne sat on the armchair near mine.

"So it must have been difficult for you all those years. You had to hide your thoughts from the other military people. After the war, you had to hide who you were and what you had been involved with from ... from everyone around you. You couldn't be close to anyone."

"That's true. The hardest thing was with Ruth. Yes, I saved her, but her baby...."

"Johann, please don't revisit this. You saved her and others. You couldn't save everyone. It wasn't in your power."

She put her hand on my shoulder and looked into my eyes.

"You are a good man, Johann. We all love you. Samuel loves you. You are part of our family."

Her words touched me and I cried openly – in front of Sam.

"My biggest fear is that you won't bring Samuel over here anymore."

"Johann ... honestly. Even if we wanted to do that, we could not. It would break the little guy's heart."

I found those words comforting.

"You know, Anne ... Samuel is the one who saved me. He was the one who brought me a new understanding. When I arrived here in America, I remained convinced of the old hatreds."

I paused to form my next words, but Anne presaged them.

"When we stepped into your life ... you probably didn't like it."

She looked into me, awaiting my reply.

"You're right," I confirmed. "I did not like it at all. I saw all Jews as evil ... something to be rid of."

Anne gasped at hearing what she had only suspected, what she had only read about. I was not a book or a lecture. I was a neighbor and I was right next to her.

"I knew that all those things were madness. Many times I found myself holding my head and silently asking, what the hell are we doing? Someone please wake us up. But everything around me accepted it as normal. So ... it went on."

"And then I came to know you. I came to know little Samuel."

I winked at him as he sat on quietly my lap.

"He showed me the light. Your son ... *saved* me."

I tousled his hair and he giggled.

"I owe him everything ... *everything*."

"Well," she said, about to leave, "as Rabbi Levi noted, I don't think you had evil in your heart. You demonstrated that during the war and after it."

She straightened her dress and opened the door.

"Deep in your heart, you resisted. Every chance you had, you saved someone. Ruth ... the little boy ... you probably can't even remember the others."

She released a long sigh and added, "Maybe there were *many* others."

"Well, I must be off. Bye sweetie. I'll pick you up after work."

She blew a kiss to Samuel but he was preoccupied with a fire engine.

"See you later, Anne. Have a pleasant day."

"So Samuel. What deeds await us on this fine morning?"

"Let's go see the horses down the street," he replied hopefully.

"Sure, I love to visit the horses."

"Yay! You saved one once. Remember?"

"Yes. I do remember. We saved that horse."
This little boy remembers everything!

The days became better. I found peace. Rabbi Levi continued his visits and taught me Jewish history and traditions. He mentioned that most in the congregation had, in time and through his counsel, accepted my confession. A few expressed reservations but he insisted that word of my past be kept within the *kehila*. If further action were called for – especially notifying the authorities – it would be done only after he and I had spoken.

Samuel was growing up and we started having deeper conversations. He once asked me if I had ever been a soldier. I replied that I had and this fascinated him.

"How many people did you save?"

I had to veer away from the subject. And I believe I will for the rest of my life.

We spent hours at the lake during his summer vacation. Samuel loves to swim and anything to do with the water, so I got him an inflatable raft big enough for the captain and his first mate. We rowed about, changing course with each passing whim.

"Aye, aye, Captain Rosenberg!"

Some nights he stayed overnight and we'd make dinner then look up at the skies. Like a doting grandfather, I bought him whatever he wanted. He was a little spoiled, but who cared. He was happy and that was the most important thing. That summer was probably the best one we ever had.

The fall was short that year and a cruel winter had set in by early December. The snow in January was calamitous, reaching two feet – more where the wind had formed drifts. Schools and even many workplaces closed. I hardly left the house. Anne still brought Samuel almost every day – mostly because he demanded it. We were just fine in my cozy house.

One wintry day Samuel told me his father was sick.

"What does he have? A cold? The flu?"

"Something real bad, I think."

He was eager to show me he had learned something, but there was deep concern on his face as well.

"Mom cried all last night. I heard them talking this morning. He's going to a hospital."

Anne did not look her best when she came for Samuel. She appeared tired and her eyes suggested she had had little sleep. I'd noticed weariness in recent days, but nothing like this. Samuel was sound asleep, giving Anne and me time to talk.

"Is everything okay, Anne?"

She only gave me a look of sadness and worry.

"Have a seat please? Can I help with something?"

She sat and exhaled, as though welcoming the chance to tell of her woe.

"Things are not going well with Elliot. He's quite ill."

"Yes, Samuel just told me this morning. May I ask the nature of his illness?"

The delay in her answer did not augur well.

"Two weeks ago, during a routine checkup, we found out that Elliot's liver has problems. Further tests showed serious malfunctioning and ... well, his liver is failing. The doctors don't know exactly why ... another mysterious virus. Medications show no signs of success. We are scheduled to visit Yale Medical Center next Friday. There are specialists there."

Complete liver failure, I knew, would be fatal.

Samuel might lose his father.

"Elliot is not at all well nowadays. He suffers from pain throughout his body and can't go to work. He's been home for more than a week. He might need a liver transplant. It's a new procedure though not as risky as it was when it first came about in the mid-sixties. I guess that wasn't so long ago. We've registered on the database and are on the waiting list. Without a transplant, Elliot may only have a month."

She had held back her tears quite well, but the last statement was too much. I held her in my arms and gently rocked her as she sobbed unashamedly.

"Anne ... Anne ... I am so sorry to hear that. But we have to think positively. There are excellent doctors at Yale. We have to be strong – and believe that he will be well again."

Anne wiped her tears with her handkerchief.

"Yes, I'm trying but it's *so* hard. I'm trying mainly for Samuel's sake. He's already noticed that his dad is sick but he doesn't know the severity. He's too young – thank heaven."

"I have great faith in medical knowledge. In the meantime, if there's anything I can help with, please let me know."

Annc looked relieved, unburdened.

"Thank you, Johann. You're so considerate – such a good person, always helping, caring and loving."

She shook her head.

"I simply cannot imagine you in … in that awful situation back then."

"Thank you, Anne. In a way, that's a wonderful compliment."

We sat there for a while as little Samuel woke up and looked around groggily.

"Time to go, Sam. Many thanks again, Johann."

She smiled bravely and with more assurance than I would have thought possible.

Samuel hugged me so tightly I actually felt a little pain in my shoulder.

"Hey, you're a big strong boy. Be more careful with an old man!"

I looked closely at his beautiful, innocent face.

"I love you, Samuel. I love you very much. I'll see you tomorrow."

"Yes, I love you too, Johann."

"Seeing you both like this breaks my heart every time. I know it's only until tomorrow … but he just loves you so much."

"We're all going to be well. Go home and be with Elliot. And you, little boy, go be with your dad. He needs your good spirits now."

I remained behind, alone. It was very hard for me to say goodbye to Samuel, even if it was only for the night. After he leaves … there is a void.

The love of a little child means everything.

The next month was a blur of events and emotions. The Yale visit led to a different series of medications but if there was any change in Elliot's condition, it was only slight or temporary. Elliot flew to Colorado to meet with Dr Singh, the Indian doctor who pioneered the liver transplant procedure. He concluded that Elliot's liver was nearing complete shutdown and that the only hope was a transplant.

The waiting list was lengthy, and furthermore there was a complication. Elliot's blood type was quite rare – so rare that a proper match would be exceedingly difficult. The doctors braced Anne and

Elliot for the possibility that he would not last long enough for a transplant.

The atmosphere at the Rosenberg home became gloomy. Anne struggled to avoid falling into depression. I moved in with them in order to help with Samuel and hired a nurse to help out.

Anne needed to go to work – for the income and to keep from sinking into despair. Rabbi Levi visited almost every day, offering spiritual support. It was hard to believe that with all of the marvels of modern medicine there was nothing that could be done. I did my own research on liver experts and hired an attorney to search for a donor – or even a seller.

The fact that a significant amount of Elliot's liver had to be replaced made things harder. Although I offered an attractive incentive to any prospect, we could not find one with Elliot's blood type. Only one percent of the population has his AB- blood type. Time was passing by.

One night I sat with Samuel on the couch, watching TV. It was getting late and Anne had fallen asleep on the rocking chair, as she had many times over the past few weeks. She was exhausted, emotionally and physically. Samuel was often the last one who went to sleep. Anne was often too weary to put him to bed. Many nights I tried to tell him stories or read to him to help him fall asleep, but with only occasional success.

"Dad is not getting better, is he."

The disarming candor shook me from my drowsing.

He knew his father was not at all well but Anne and I agreed to keep the atmosphere optimistic though. But Samuel was a smart lad and could see things weren't right. It was clear from his parents' words and emotions and their strained explanations to him. Nurses, frequent trips, phone calls, concerned glances – they all added up in his mind.

"No Sam, he's not getting better yet. The doctors are still working at it though."

"That is why mom is upset." he concluded.

His eyes saddened before me.

"Yes, these are hard times for all of us."

Samuel was deep in thought.

"Johann, what's dad's problem?"

"Well, his liver – it works with your stomach – is not working well."

"So what are they going to do now?"

"Well, we'd like to get your dad a liver *transplant*."

"What's that?"

"That's when someone gives his liver to someone who needs a liver. Doctors will put the other liver into your father. With the new liver, your dad will be just fine."

"Like fixing a car? Dad told me once that we had to replace a part in our car. Then the car worked fine."

"Exactly," I confirmed. "Like a new part inside a car. Only this time it's inside your dad's tummy."

Samuel mulled this over while he took in a little television. Then another question occurred.

"So can't we just go get another liver?"

"It's not that easy to find one. It has to come from somebody."

I was debating how to explain to him that the donor is usually dead – a word I was reluctant to use.

"Then the liver has to be a good match for your father. Your dad can't use just any old liver! Your dad needs a big liver and one with the right blood type."

This was a bit over his head and I was happy for that. Going deeper into medical matters could only cause deeper worries. No more questions, I hoped.

"What's a blood type?"

No luck.

"Every person has a blood type, A, B, O and so on. Some people have a different blood type; some have the same blood type. Your dad's new liver must come from someone with the same blood type. That way, the liver will work just fine with your dad."

"What happens to the guy who gives the liver?"

No luck again.

"The liver comes from someone who has died. That is the only way we can take the liver. For example, if someone dies in a car accident then he does not need his liver anymore. The doctor can give his liver to your father."

Samuel thought for a second.

"So the liver's donor has to be dead somehow."

"Yes, he does.... You are such a smart boy!"

Samuel seemed to have some grasp of the concept.

"Your father," I continued, "has an unusual blood type. It's very hard to find a person who has his blood type and who can give away his liver."

I heaved a long sigh.

"This is our main problem now...."

Samuel did not hear my last comment. He was already asleep. I sat there in silence as Sam and his mom dozed.

What a cruel world. Here is a wonderful father of an amazing child and he has a rare disease and an even rarer blood type. It's just not fair. Life is not fair.

My mind wandered into my past – into my dark past, where I was loth to go.

Waffen SS soldiers had their blood types tattooed onto their left arm, but I was in the other part of the SS and we had no such mark. Still, wasn't our blood type on our identity discs and pay books? Bah! I couldn't remember, and in any case I destroyed all those things long ago. Or else they were souvenirs of a Russian foot soldier.

During the preparation for Plan O they ran extensive blood tests on all candidates....

A glimmer of an old memory flashed through my mind.

I remember some difficulties with me. What was the issue? It was something with my blood type.

What is my blood type?

The next morning I scheduled a medical checkup.

The results were in some sense good. I was in fine health.

"You are a healthy man. Whatever you're doing, keep doing it. I hope I'm in such good shape when I get to be your age," the doctor reported cheerfully.

I wasn't terribly interested in my health let alone his upbeat chatter.

"Oh, and here are the values for your cholesterol ... blood pressure ... white blood count ... blood type...."

Elliot's condition was deteriorating rapidly. He was unable to function very much and he remained in bed. The doctors had run out of options. Elliot needed an immediate transplant – no more than two weeks. We were all devastated.

One night Samuel sat on my lap again and watched television as I meandered between consciousness and sleep.

"Turn off the television, Johann," he exclaimed to my astonishment. "I don't want to watch anymore."

I pulled him close and we rocked back and forth for a while.

"I heard mom crying today. When I asked her what's wrong, she told me that dad may not be with us for long ... and we have to prepare for that.... Is he going to die, Johann?"

I did not answer right away.

"If a matched liver is not be found on time, he may not be with us very long. Yes, we have to prepare for that."

I could not lie to him.

"But I don't want him to die."

Samuel cried and wiped his eyes.

"No one wants your father to die." I answered softly. "Your father also does not want to die. It's beyond our powers. Some things are greater than us. Some things we have no control over."

His tearful eyes made me feel helpless.

Many anguishing thoughts passed through my mind that night. By early morning, I had made my decision.

"I have an idea," I told Anne over breakfast.

Though only twenty-nine, the ravages of worry and desperation had been most unkind to her. My words raised a little hope and I did not want to raise false hope.

"I need to go for a while today," I added.

"Sure, I'll be here," she replied flatly.

I scheduled an urgent appointment with my doctor and calmly apprised him of my new plan. As I expected, he was taken aback. I asked him the odds of success and he said he'd do some research and have an estimate in twenty-four hours.

He called the next day with good news – ninety percent chance of success for the recipient, but the donor's chances ... not so good. He said that consent forms and legal releases would be required. That was all I wanted to hear.

"Are you out of your mind?" Anne said, staring at me wide-eyed.

It was the most life I'd seen in her for quite some time. I welcomed it.

"We don't have many options at this point, Anne. Nor do we have much time. Elliot and I have the same AB- blood type. There aren't many of us, I assure you."

"We all appreciate your offer, but it's simply not anything we can accept."

"Anne, think about Samuel. He will have a chance to grow within his loving family – mother *and* father. Think of him ... not me."

She shook her head silently.

"I understand that ... and I appreciate your concern. A donor is a dead person, not a live one. We love you, Johann. We simply can't do that. Your offer is very generous, very noble ... but it's just not right. You can't sacrifice your life for Elliot's."

"Anne," I took her hand in mine, "This is my chance to do good – atonement."

"Johann, you didn't have any choice then, but you have choice now – and so do I. My answer is no!"

Anne sank back into exhaustion, unable to summon any more arguments against me. I tried to take advantage of that. I looked into her weary, hopeless eyes with all the authority I had left.

"Just let me handle things, Anne. Everything will work out."

"No! With my last strength I am telling you, I will not agree to this."

"Anne, there's a reasonable chance I'll survive the procedure. My entire liver might not be required – sometimes only part of a donor's organ is needed. In this way, there's a chance that I will live and Elliot will live as well." I added carefully, "I'll gladly take the chance."

She did not answer, so I pressed on.

"I'm in very good health. My chance of survival is quite good for a man my age."

I held her hand firmly.

"I *want* to do it."

She did not answer. It was too much for her. She went to her room. Sam was sound asleep and blissfully unaware of the debate that was going on.

The doctor had told me that my chances were slim. "Almost no chance," was how he put it. "Don't even consider it."

I told him to keep that between him and me.

"No one else needs to know."

I thought through the arrangements I needed to take care of. There were many legal ones involving property. Others were of a personal, spiritual sort.

It was Thursday night. I looked at my watch – almost midnight. Next Monday was the date for the transplant.

The next morning, after a quick breakfast, I stopped Anne as she was leaving for work. She looked exhausted – barely able to think.

"Anne, I have something to talk with you about."

She looked at me quizzically, though only for a moment.

"I would like to leave tomorrow for Cape Cod. I'll be back on Sunday, about noon. Can I take little Samuel with me, please?"

"Sure. It would be good for him to get away for a day or two."

"Also, with your permission, I would like to arrange Elliot's liver transplant for next Monday."

She shook her head silently almost before my inevitable point was made.

"Anne, Samuel saved my life. Without him I would never have had a reason to live. He saved my soul and I want to give him a gift. I have a chance now to give him a very precious gift – his father."

I looked into her eyes, trying silently to convince her to agree. I do not know what thoughts passed through her mind, but after a painful silence she faintly nodded before she could bring herself to speak.

"It's ultimately your decision ... and I will respect it, Johann," she answered softly.

"Thank you, Anne. You did the right thing. You'll have to sign some papers so we can move forward with the operation. We don't have much time. It's set for Monday."

Anne left with Samuel and I remained in their home. I had many things to do that day. One of them was to get pen and paper to continue my journal.

After the legal folderol, everything was ready. It's a complicated procedure, with many incisions and a lot of suturing, so three surgeons and one anesthesiologist were called in. One of the surgeons – the fellow in Colorado – was being flown in and would arrive Sunday afternoon.

Since most of my liver would be removed, I might have only a few days afterwards. During that time I'd be in the best room in the hospital – the one you need to have connections to get.

I attended the Friday evening service at the synagogue. A relentless rain kept many away that night. Rabbi Levi was very happy to see me. I chose not tell him of my decision.

"I hear that Elliot's condition is not so good," he noted sadly.

"Oh … you haven't heard. We found a donor," I told him cheerfully. "The surgery will be on Monday. The doctor says Elliot's chances are quite good."

"Great news! This, I did not know."

"Yes, it came up only yesterday. There is hope."

"We should all pray tonight for Elliot's health."

"Absolutely! I'll be joining you tonight in the prayers."

Well into the service, Rabbi Levi requested prayers for Elliot.

"On this Shabbat I would like to say a special prayer for a precious member of our *kehila* – Elliot Rosenberg. Elliot has been stricken with liver trouble and has been fighting for his life over the past months. Without a transplant, he will leave us. Only quite recently have the doctors found a suitable donor for him. Monday, he will undergo liver transplant surgery. The doctors are optimistic – and so should we. I would like us all to say a prayer for Elliot."

"Thank you, Rabbi Levi," Anne said as she stood up in the second row.

All eyes turned to her.

"I would like to add one piece of information pertinent to the operation."

She looked over to me then continued. I knew what was coming.

"The donor of Elliot's new liver is here with us this evening. He is Johann Kraus."

I closed my eyes as whispers rushed through the room. Rabbi Levi looked at me in astonishment and wonder.

"Yes, Johann has volunteered to give his liver to Elliot … to Samuel's father.… He is in good health and has the same rare blood type as Elliot. Since almost his entire liver will be given to Elliot, his chances are not good. I know … I talked with a doctor regarding the matter. His chances, in fact, are slim," Anne added in a surprisingly strong voice.

Many in the congregation turned to me.

"As Johann is now a member of the *kehila*, I thought we should all know what sort of man we've had among us."

There was a heavy silence in the synagogue as people thought her words through. Because so many eyes were on me, I felt I had to say something. I stood, as I had not too long before for quite another reason.

"The Rosenbergs are my family. I never imagined that I'd feel like this.... Well, you know my story. You know who I was then ... and I hope you see who I am now. Still it cannot take away the evil I took part in. It does not matter what one thinks or says, eventually it is the soul that cries out, the conscience that does not forget – and more than that, does not forgive.

"Now I have the opportunity to do something good for the family that showed me the proper path – the path of righteousness. The family that brought me happiness I never thought I'd have.

"I tried to find a donor. I hired the best people to conduct a search. I did everything in my powers to give the Rosenbergs continued happiness. I'll do anything for them, even if it means giving my life. For all the people whose deaths I participated in, I would like to give this one life I have. There is a moment in a man's life when he feels he can make a difference. This is my moment."

Only a little shuffling interrupted the silence. Then Rabbi Levi's powerful voice sounded.

"I would like us to say a prayer for Elliot and for Johann. Two respected and loved members of our congregation."

All rose.

And so the rabbi led a prayer for both of us. His voice was loud and he paced about with strength and dedication. He recited this prayer as he never had before and the congregation's participation was never fuller.

Such passion....

His eyes did not move from the prayer book until the final words came from him and the *kehila*. He came to me and shook my hand.

"Thank you for the prayer, Rabbi Levi," I told him. "It was quite moving."

"You're welcome," his eyes glistened with tears. "You are a good man, Johann Kraus."

"Thank you.… You are all good people. And it was my honor and privilege to meet each of you."

He used his handkerchief to dry his eyes then left for his study. There was so much to think about. So much.

The next morning Sam and I were off to Cape Cod. A beautiful morning promised a beautiful day. The ride was pleasant and soon enough we were in Chatham. Sam raced to the shore while I followed behind more leisurely. I was in no hurry. We took off our shoes and socks and let the water flow over our feet. Was it my imagination or was the water a bit warm for this time of year?

We ambled along the shoreline and watched the large tankers and container ships sail off on the horizon, on their way to New York or London – maybe even Hamburg. Seagulls glided about overhead and squawked for a morsel to eat from the people below. From time to time we could see a jetliner descending on its approach to Boston's Logan airport. It was an enchanting day. The salty air formed a haze on the horizon into which the ships sailed before disappearing entirely. I suppose it was always like that but I'd not noticed it.

I thought about Hamburg.

"Do you like it here, Samuel?" I asked with a wistful smile.

"I love it here. It's the most beautiful place in the world," he declared just as an unusually high wave brought ocean water almost to our knees.

"That's great!" he roared with laughter.

I played along.

"I wish my mom and dad were like you and took me here a lot."

"Well, I'll mention it to them. How's that sound?"

"Super!"

"You know, Samuel … you're my best friend."

"I know," he said matter-of-factly. "You're my best friend … but you know that already."

"Yes, thank you. I do know that but it's always nice to hear it from a loved one."

I did not know how to start this discussion. I looked out to an ocean liner all but gone from sight.

"Samuel, you're a big boy now...."

"Yes, I am," came his proud answer.

Things may be harder on me than on him. Children take events as they are.

"You know, your dad is having an operation on Monday. The doctors think he'll be just fine and he'll return to you and your mom soon enough."

"Yes, mom told me that yesterday. We will all be together again. Mom will be very happy ... but she cried when she said that. She said it's all thanks to you because you found the liver. Thanks a million, Johann."

"You're welcome. Let's walk a little more."

"Good idea. I love the warm sand on bare feet!"

I breathed the salty sea air deep into my lungs. Too deeply. I had to cough a bit.

"I have to tell you something important," I said after a hundred yards or so.

"What is it?"

"You know that sometimes we have to make very hard decisions in our lives."

His eyebrows furrowed in puzzlement and maybe a little trepidation as well. We stopped and sat on the sand together, side by side.

"I love you, Samuel."

"Why are you crying, Johann?"

Such a painful question.

"What's wrong?"

"I would like to tell you something as a grownup. Do you think you can handle that, my friend?"

"Of course I can."

I had to get to the matter.

"On Monday I am going to give my liver to your dad. I have the same blood type that he has and that will work best for him."

He looked at me, knowing there was more.

"Your dad will have a new liver and he will get better within a week or two. That's very good news. The bad news is that I will not have a liver anymore."

I let him think about that awhile.

"Oh.… So what will they do with you? Are you going to get a new liver from someone else?"

"No, there are no more donors. Remember I said that your father and I have an unusual blood type?"

"Oh, yes.… What's this mean for you? How you are going to do without your liver?"

The hard part.

"We don't know yet," I told him gently. "There is some chance that I will get better … but it's only a very small chance. Within a few days, maybe a week but not much more, I might die."

He seemed confused for a moment. I knew he would think this through.

"Why?"

"Because no one can go without a liver."

He looked down into the millions of grains of sand with a hurt look.

"But I don't want you to die, Johann."

He started to cry and I pressed him to my heart.

"I know Samuel … but we have to save your dad. You see, you have to grow up with a father. You love your father, don't you?"

He nodded.

"So … in this way you can grow up with your father – in a happy family. I decided to tell you that so you would not be mad at me if I left suddenly. We have to tell the truth to the people we love."

"But.…" He was confused and sad and had difficulties finding his words.

"It makes good sense. I am no longer young and do not have too much longer to live anyway. Your father is still young and you need him for many years to come."

"You're giving your liver to dad so that he can live, but you have to die.… That's not fair. I want you both."

The pain of a child who thinks he faces the decision of choosing between people he loves. Long ago people had to face situations like this almost daily. Mothers had to choose between their children, give away their babies.... The pain of those memories was weaker then.

Samuel wrapped his little arm around my neck. He did not speak. He simply held me and held me. I cried because I was saying goodbye to my best friend. I cried because my days of seeing his smiling face were growing short. I cried because I was losing my dearest friend – my dearest friend and my savior.

We spent two beautiful days on the beach. We waded into the ocean, ran on the beach and gazed at the magnificent stars that shone brightly so far from the lights of Boston. We did not dwell on matters. Samuel wanted to enjoy every minute of our weekend. I was glad that he knew the truth.

It was our best time together, ever. All in all, Samuel took the news quite well.

Brave boy....

"Time to head back home, my friend."

It was Sunday afternoon and we were having ice cream at a small café near the beach.

"Yes, I know...."

His expression darkened.

"You'll have to remember to ask your mom and dad to come here with you. And I'll tell them, of course. It's such a beautiful place, isn't it."

"Yes, I'll remember.... I'll tell them that this is *our* place."

"That's right ... *our* place. You are my brave boy. You know, Samuel, you're going to grow up, go to college and be an adult one day. Always be kind to other people. Respect their beliefs and ways of life. Respect their freedom and choices. I did not always do so in the past ... many years ago...."

He looked at me with curiosity

"But you are a good man."

"Well, back then … long ago. Today I am very sorry for those things. I wish I could turn back the wheels of time…. I would live my life very differently."

He took my hand.

"Do not worry, Johann. You're a good man now. It does not matter what you did many years ago. You are good today … and that is what is important."

"Thank you, Samuel…."

We finished our ice cream and looked out onto the deep blue ocean and the far horizon. It seemed to beckon me.

Life for Life

Dr Singh had come in from Colorado the day before and prepared for the procedure. He made a better calculation of the amount of my liver that would be needed. The word was not final; that would only be known with certainty after the surgery. The estimate wasn't good but I was expecting that. I was aware that after I woke up – if I woke up – I might have only a short time to live. I will, by my own request, be in Ruth's room.

"How do you feel?" Dr Singh asked.

"I'm well … and ready. Thank you for the information."

"Elliot is in the next room. In a moment we will bring you in and start the incisions."

He spoke in a cool, professional manner. Maybe it was the only way he could handle this situation.

I nodded with confidence – most of it feigned. I felt as ready as I ever would.

Samuel and Anne came in to wish me the best.

Samuel took my hand without saying anything. Anne wiped her tears quietly. I asked them to wait for me in the room. I wanted to live as long as I could for one reason. Having said my goodbyes to Samuel, I wanted to see that Elliot was recovering.

"I love you, Samuel. Always remember that."

"I love you too, Johann – very much," he whispered. He waved goodbye as I was wheeled away.

I was taken into a brightly-lit operating room, one with seating above for students and observers. I was positioned next to Elliot.

"Are you ready, Johann?"

The question abruptly halted my thoughts.

I saw Samuel's gentle face looking from a seat above. And I smiled.

He will be with me. How lovely.

"Yes, I am ready...."

Aftermath

"JOHANN ... JOHANN ..."

I heard a familiar voice but was too weak to talk. When I slowly opened my eyes I saw my reason for being there.

I also saw many tubes protruding from me and strange machines all around me. It was too complicated to comprehend just then. I closed my eyes and returned to my dark slumber.

Sometime later, I woke up again. Samuel was still there, as was the surgeon.

"Johann, how are you?" a voice asked.

The worried face of Dr Singh formed out of a haze.

"I've been better," I groggily stated.

I surprised myself. I still had the capacity for witticisms. In that same vein, I though to myself that the "O" in Plan O now stood for "Operation." Weird what I am thinking about in such moments, a thought crossed my mind.

I sensed that my entire body was largely numb and worse, almost paralyzed. I wasn't as well as I had thought. I closed my eyes and mumbled largely incoherently.

"Yes, yes. I know what you mean!" the surgeon quipped.

At least I managed to get a smile from him. But after that it was all business.

"Here's the situation. As I suspected, we had to remove almost all of your liver.... This, I'm afraid, does not bode well ... not well at all."

"I can sense that," I answered slowly. Every word required enormous effort.

He nodded.

"There are medications, of course ... but it's out of our hands. Let me know if we can help you with anything."

With that, he left the room.

"How's your dad doing?" I asked Samuel.

"They don't know. Mom is with him now.... She'll be here soon."

I looked around the room and it became familiar. The wide windows brought in generous amounts of morning light, which flooded the room and seemed to cleanse and purify it of anything bad.

"Beautiful sunshine ... I am truly glad to see you, Samuel."

"Yes, very beautiful."

He held my hand and I was as happy as any human can be, regardless of health.

All my life I had been in good health. Not now. Now I felt very weak. I could sense that something was wrong. There was a constant, dull pain in my abdomen and a strange feeling I had never experienced – something....

Anne entered the room and greeted me and made the usual inquiries. But my concerns were not with me.

"How is Elliot?" I asked, conjuring a smile.

"He's at a critical stage of acceptance or rejection of ... your liver. We'll know in the next hour or so. They worked on you both almost all night."

"Don't worry about me. I'll be fine."

"Rest, Johann. You need to rest. Your pen and paper are right here."

"Yes," I mumbled and soon I was again in deep sleep.

I saw Ruth. Yes, it was a familiar place. A dark place. It was a camp. Treblinka. Ruth ... and that cruel officer – Schaffer. We were all standing in the selection yard. Something different. Ruth held her baby in her arms. Sara was wrapped in a pure white cloth. I felt panic ... a kind of panic that few men know. Schaffer was about to kill the baby. Not memory ... I am here this time. I am here and I am in charge. In a surreal motion, I draw my pistol and shove it into Schaffer's chest.

"Do not move an inch until I say so!"

Ruth smiled serenely.

"There is no need for that, Johann. See? My baby is well. Sara is well."

She smiled and showed me a beautiful tiny baby slumbering safely at her mother's breast.

Everyone stood still and looked on at the scene. For an instant, we were in a deep forest – lush greens, not cold grays. I couldn't understand what was happening.

"All is well, Johann ... all is well."

I slowly lowered my pistol from Schaffer's chest.

We stood once more in the selection yard, but all was peaceful.

Ruth held her baby and slowly rocked her to sleep. Neither Schaffer nor any of the soldiers moved. They simply stood there looking on – frozen in time, frozen in the past. I relaxed and holstered my pistol.

Ruth smiled. And I was happy.

We were together, there in the pastoral glory that God granted us, with the stars shining over us.

I woke up, perspiring heavily. I was hot ... burning up. A nurse was moistening my forehead with a cold cloth.

"You have a fever and we are working on it," the nurse said with a forced smile.

"It was anticipated," the doctor added as he reentered the room. "Your liver function is near zero. We're giving you steroids to help stave off infection."

I nodded as best I could.

I looked down and there he was. Little Samuel sat there looking up at me ... smiling lovingly.

"Hi Johann...."

As fine a welcome as I could recall.

"How are you, my friend?"

Samuel stood and held my hand.

"Wow, you're very warm!"

"Yes ... I have a fever ... but it'll soon pass."

Try to be confident.

"How is dad?" I asked between alternate chills and heat flashes.

"The doctors say we will know soon. Mom is with him all the time."

"He'll be fine. Let me know of any change."

"Sure. Would you like me to bring you something?"

"I am good for now. You're a good boy, Samuel – and I love you."

"You don't look that well, Johann," he told me with a sad look.

The blunt candor of children!

"I look exactly how I feel!"

I did not feel well at all. I was cold and hot – sometimes at the same time. The nurse assured me that the medicine would soon kick-in, and I was looking forward to that so that I could do a little more writing.

I reached to him and held his hand. I did not have the power to continue talking. Samuel felt it and did not talk anymore.

The medicine did indeed kick in. My chills slowly disappeared and my fever got under control. I felt exhausted though. Soon enough I fell asleep.

When I woke, the fever was gone. No one was in the room. Only then did I see that there were flowers arranged on the nightstand and windowsill.

The congregation....

It was sunset and the room was illuminated by orange sunbeams. The window was open a bit and a breeze sent a pine scent into the room.

Ruth and I shared a sunset like this not long ago. I yearn to be with her once more.

I looked back on my life and thought about the various decisions I had made – during the war, after the war, and my most recent one. *My final one.*

I was pleased with that one. I saved a family, the most precious family for me, my true family – here in America.

Something was wrong with my body. It was failing, breaking down.

The end is coming.

Not yet, though. I have to see that Elliot pulls through. Only then can I let go.

I breathed in the pine-scented air. It gave me strength. I felt well for a while. I even did a little writing.

"Good evening, Mr Kraus," the nurse said on entering my room. "Are you up for a little something to eat tonight?"

"Water only, please," I replied hoarsely.

"Coming right up. Just let me know if you'll need anything else."

She smiled courteously and left the room.

Evening fell and the last light of the day was gone. Would I see tomorrow's sun? The dull abdominal pain was spreading throughout my body. My arm was getting weak and I don't know how much longer I can write.

I awoke in the early morning. The night had been uncomfortable.

I am going to die soon. I watched so many people die before but never imagined the feeling. Fast or slow.... My time is almost here but I am not yet ready.

Elliot.

I called the nurse.

"Can you see if the little boy is around, please?"

"Samuel? Yes, he just got here. His mom took him in to see his dad. Good news – Mr Rosenberg woke up and is feeling remarkably well, all things considered."

"That's splendid news – exactly what I wanted to hear."

"Samuel will be right along," the nurse added. "Anything else I can help you with?"

"No, thank you."

I smiled to her. She was a pleasant young black woman.

"You know … I think my time has come…."

She fell silent with genuine concern.

"Oh! I'll call Dr Singh. He – "

"No, please," I stopped her. "There is no need. It was anticipated."

I held her hand.

"Can you stay with me, please?"

When one's time comes … it's often unsettling. I looked at her. She had good eyes. I saw tears welling up.

"You should not be so emotional. This is a hospital … and people die here all the time!"

"Yes … true. I'm sorry."

I read her last name on her ID card – Johnson.

"Miss Johnson…. May I know your first name?'

"Yes, of course. It's Mildred."

"Ahh…. Mildred."

She held my hand. Even a short time together can lead to human ties.

What an irony. Someone who despised Jews, blacks and other minorities, is going to end his life with them.

But I've changed. I'm very glad that I've changed. My soul found truth. I was able to see right and wrong, good and bad. This is the best way that I could end my life. I learned to see many things. I had to see the tragic error in my life – and in many people. It was an error that played a role in killing millions. I don't know what awaits me, but I cannot expect a heavenly reward. Punishment is waiting, and I'm prepared for it.

I deserve it.

"Johann, dad is going to be fine!"

Samuel burst into the room, climbed onto my bed and hugged me.

Although quite weak, I was the happiest man on earth. I looked to Mildred.

"Thank you for staying with me until my friend came along."

Mildred smiled as she turned to leave. Anne came in as Mildred was going out.

"He's awake! The vital signs are quite good and his body seems to be accepting the new liver – *your* liver. Thank you ever so very much…. But how do you feel?"

Her joy gave way to worry. I just nodded with a weak smile.

"Oh!"

Anne's hand went to her mouth.

"Oh no…." Samuel whispered.

I hugged him as Anne silently wept.

"I want to tell you that you were my only family – my beloved family. I was blessed to have you in my life. You were my light after so much darkness."

Dr Singh entered the room and made routine but irrelevant checks.

"I can put you on some medication that may – "

"No, thank you. It is, as you know, a natural process. The pain is not strong. I will fall asleep soon."

Dr Singh wanted to say something but chose not to.

"Anne," I asked in a weak voice, "can you call Rabbi Levi, please?"

"I don't want you to die!" Samuel sobbed.

"This was all known to us, my friend. I am no longer a young man. That is the way of all things."

Grand discourses on the nature of the world were of little interest to Sam. He simply hugged me.

"I love you, Samuel. I could not have loved you more had you been my own son. You will forever be in my heart."

Samuel lay near me as Anne cried silently.

"There is never a good time for loved ones to die," Anne whispered.

"Just let me know if I can help with something," Dr Singh said.

He leaned down to me and whispered, "It's been an inspiration to know you."

"Johann, I am here."

It was Rabbi Levi. Science had left the room, religion had come in. I asked him to complete my journal.

Why have these people loved me? I've changed … This is larger than I am … I'll be judged by a greater power….

"Is there anything that you want to tell me?" The rabbi saw my difficulties and tried to help me.

"I just wanted the people I love … and are the most precious to me … to be with me in my last moments."

"We are here."

I nodded and smiled faintly.

"You know, Johann, the heavens have mercy. You also did good things – you saved people. When you face your final judgment, you will see light, not darkness."

I could barely move.

"First I'll face punishment, I think … Maybe after that, I'll see light … maybe."

"I'm sure you will."

Rabbi Levi held my hand in his.

"I'll pray for you," he added.

I thought I saw tears in his eyes.

Samuel had fallen asleep next to me … and I was glad for that.

"Rabbi…."

"Yes Johann, I am here."

"I actually do have a last wish."

"What is it, my friend?"

He leaned close to me to hear my failing voice.

"It's something I've long wanted to request … but never did."

"I'll do everything I can."

"Do you remember the rabbi that said the Kaddish for his slain students? I told you this story, didn't I?"

"Yes, I remember that man quite well…."

"Promise me...."

"Yes, Johann?"

"... that you will still say a Kaddish prayer for him."

Rabbi Levi was surprised, moved, even taken aback by the request.

"You know, when I saw him saying this prayer for his students ... I asked him, 'Who is going to say the prayer for you?' but he never answered."

I gathered more strength and continued.

"He did not have anyone to say the prayer for him ... I wanted to say the prayer for him ... I truly did."

Rabbi Levi was deeply moved as the meaning of the request sunk in.

"I could not say it, of course ... I was ... one of them ... besides ... I did not know the words. I never forgot that rabbi ... that holy man who prayed for everyone else ... but who had no one to say a prayer over him.... Can you say a prayer for him, please?"

"Of course. I promise to say the prayer for him – at the next service."

"Thank you, Rabbi Levi....Now I know someone ... a good man ... will read the Kaddish for him."

"What was his name? What was the rabbi's name?"

"His name was Rabbi Mordechai," I answered with a weak smile.

He nodded and smiled, too.

"Rabbi Mordechai. A strong name."

My vision blurred and dimmed. A peculiar taste came to my mouth. I could not feel my body anymore. I heard Samuel talking but I was too weak to understand. The doctor reappeared and looked at my eyes with the help of a small flashlight.

The doctor looked at Rabbi Levi and Anne with a meaningful look. Then he left the room. I sensed Samuel. He was close to me. He was talking to me. I could not hear him well, but I willed my arms to hug him. I held him to my heart and it felt good to have him near me.

"I promise, Johann. I'll say the prayer for him," Rabbi Levi said.

I looked around at the faces of the people I loved and respected. Everyone seemed ready.

I did not expect forgiveness. I have a chance for the light.

I am ready.

I closed my eyes and told Rabbi Levi what I hoped awaited me, what I hoped I'd see in a little while.

The room would become a long, dark tunnel. No light. I peer ahead of me, hoping to see a glimmer of light but cannot. Only darkness. I anticipated this. I hoped for light … I hoped for light.

Samuel!

My imagination? No. Samuel is standing there. I want to hold him but he is too far. I reach for him but my arms do not heed me. Just the same, I am happy to see him there with me.

He points ahead. "Me?" I ask. He nods and beckons me on. I walk towards him and deeper into the inky tunnel. I fear what lies ahead but Samuel calms me. He again points ahead but once more I see only darkness. He continues to point and now I see something. Far away in the distance, barely discernible, I see it.

A single point of light. Infinitesimally small, yet clearly there ahead of us.

There is light for me at the end of this.

Samuel smiles and I am euphoric. "Will you come with me into the tunnel?" I ask without any motion or word or sound. He continues to point ahead, as he always has. I am certain he will be with me all the way to the light.

My heart fills with boundless gratitude. I will not be alone. I'll pass through this dark tunnel and Samuel will be with me until I reach the light. I am grateful. Goodness counts. Darkness ends.

Good prevails.

Samuel motions that we need to continue.

I place my hand in his and together we walk down the tunnel.

Together we walk toward a light that we know will burn eternally.

Rabbi Levi's Epilogue

I, RABBI LEVI, WAS deep in thought as I paced back and forth in front of the *kehila*. Only after several minutes did I notice all the whispering and moving about. Those sounds of discomfort and perplexity told me that the congregation was eager to hear my words.

"I apologize for the delay," I noted sheepishly. "You all remember our congregation member Johann Kraus – the extraordinary man who told us his life story on Holocaust Remembrance Day."

A commotion passed through the congregation. Everyone remembered Johann from that day, though not all of them had been at the service where Johann's sacrifice had been noted, or had heard of that emotional night from those who had been there.

There had been mixed opinion on what to do about the strange case of Johann Kraus, but everyone heeded my urging to keep the confession within the community. Many there that day wanted to recommend turning him in to the authorities. Most, however, respected their rabbi's view, which I assured them had come only after considerable thought and prayer. Almost everyone there expected me to speak to the matter during the service.

"Johann underwent surgery last week in order to donate his liver to Elliot Rosenberg."

There was silence throughout the chamber as people wondered what this had to do with anything. No one murmured or asked around. All eyes were on the speaker.

"Johann passed away last night," I continued. "He passed away ... in saving Elliot. He passed away saving an entire family. And because of his decency, the Rosenbergs will remain a family and hopefully bring new members into this congregation and into this world. Blessings!

"I don't think he ever rid himself entirely of the guilt over his actions during the war, though it is my sincerest hope that in his last moments he found some way to free himself of his guilt. Johann was a good man."

I paused and let the congregation think through my account of events.

"In one of his operations, he was ordered to rid a Polish village of Jews. There was a small Jewish community there, led by a local rabbi with several Yeshiva students. The SS gathered all the Jews in the town square ... and shot them down. Only the rabbi remained alive. He asked Johann to grant him the time to say a Kaddish prayer for his dead students who lay on the ground all about him.

"Johann asked the prayer's meaning. The rabbi replied that it was a prayer of mourning. Something struck Johann inside – he was moved by this. Something compelled Johann to recognize the beauty and simplicity and sacredness of our mourning prayer. He allowed the rabbi to say his Kaddish – to *finish* his Kaddish – before a soldier shot him."

I looked over the congregation. All eyes were transfixed.

"Johann never forgot that day. Throughout his life he felt guilty for allowing his soldiers to kill that rabbi. Understanding the meaning of the Kaddish prayer, Johann was tortured by this memory for his entire life. What bothered him most was that there was no one to say the Kaddish for the rabbi himself. Johann always remembered the man's name – Rabbi Mordechai ... Rabbi Mordechai, the chief rabbi in a small Polish village long ago. I myself did not know this man's name until Johann whispered it into my ear ... only moments before he passed away.

"Johann thought about something – was tormented by something – something that many would have forgotten or refused to think about. Johann thought about the brave rabbi and about the prayer that should have been said for him. Before Johann died he asked me one favor. It was not something for him. Nor was it for anyone here with us on this day.

"His last request was for me to say a prayer .... for Rabbi Mordechai. He asked me to say the Kaddish prayer ... for that rabbi. That remarkable rabbi who mourned his students but had no one to mourn for him. Johann wanted to say the prayer for the rabbi that day, but he could not – for obvious reasons. He did not know how ... and he would have been killed by his soldiers."

I released a long sigh.

"I will now say the next prayer for Rabbi Mordechai, who mourned his students and friends ... without anyone to mourn him. As was Johann's last request. I now say the Kaddish for that man."

And so I then started to recite the Kaddish. The entire synagogue joined me.

Samuel's Epilogue

IT WAS A COLD, gray day in Webster. A light rain fell gently on a group of people who had gathered for the memorial service. The cemetery was in the rolling countryside just outside town, near a wooded area that children played in. There was a young family, a rabbi and a handful of others.

"We gather here today," Rabbi Levi began in a strong voice, "to remember a special person whom we all knew, a man who was very precious to us. This man served in the army of darkness, but his soul always contained light. A man who ably showed his humanity where there was very little. This man was Johann Kraus.

"The man we knew was a good person. We heard his life story. He confessed it to us one day. We heard of many evil things. We heard of many good things. We heard about his torment.

"At the end of everyone's life, there is a judgment. That is the time when a greater power than we take account one's good and bad actions in this world.

"We humans see with our eyes, the Lord sees inside our souls."

Rabbi Levi paused and looked about at the bowed heads.

"On this day, as with every year, we are witnessing again the greater power's judgment and observation about souls and spirits. After mortality asserts itself, the spirit leaves our world and moves forward. The judgment is not known to us. So it is rare to feel any certainty about the fate of a soul.

"Even if we think we truly know a person, there are aspects of his life and actions that we do not know. As I said, by our human limitations, we can judge only by what we see and hear. In Johann's case, however, it might be clear what the judgment is. We have a sign every year when we conduct this service. It is a sign sent us, a sign that we are right in our thoughts of this man ... a sign to the world that this person symbolizes what we engraved on his headstone."

All eyes turned to Johann's grave. It positively radiated spirituality, it created an aura around it. No one had planted flowers near the site in years, nonetheless there were bright flowers and rich foliage, which gave a pastoral feeling there. Flowers of all color and description thrived there, endowing the site with too many colors to note. Those nearby breathed in the rich scents. The grave seemed to give of itself to the entire world, even on somber days like that one.

"At first we brought flowers," an old woman said to a friend. "Then we noticed that they weren't necessary. The grave has ... oh, I don't know ... its own flowers – very beautiful ones, as though this man was a precious part of creation."

She wiped her tears.

I stepped forward that day and touched the simple headstone.

"He was my best friend ... since I was a baby. He loved me as a grandfather would – even more. He taught me morals and virtues – but more than anything, he gave me my father back. He inspired me to write of our experiences together. So precious, so essential, so memorable, were they.

"My father was almost taken away, but Johann saw that he remained with me – at the price of his own life. Life for life. I'll never forget you, Johann. I love you and I hope to walk with you again."

I stood near the headstone silently.

My father stepped forward and touched the headstone.

"You gave me life in exchange for your own. There is nothing greater one can do for another. You saved a man and a family you loved. My son grew up with his father and rose to a position of respect. You saved us all. We will always be your family. You will always be in our hearts."

Rabbi Levi spoke once more. He approached the grave and put a pebble on the headstone.

"I can state the names of the people you saved. I can talk of the people you rescued when you left your estate to a foundation that aided the homeless. I can talk of our congregation and myself. We are all honored to have known you. When I met you I saw a tortured soul – one carrying a heavy burden in secret. I never imagined that your life had known such horrors. I witnessed how your soul struggled with your past and how your good heart won out. We never learned your real name ... but for us you are Johann Kraus, a man with morals and love, a man who put others before himself, a man we loved.

"I know you were not Jewish ... but your last request was for the mourning prayer to be said for a slain rabbi in Poland. I will say a mourning prayer for you now, Johann. I know you were reluctant to embrace Judaism, but now I would like to say a Kaddish for you."

All bowed silently as Rabbi Levi began the ancient prayer.

Glorified and sanctified be God's great name throughout the world which He has created according to His will. May He establish His kingdom in your lifetime and during your days, and within the life of the entire House of Israel, speedily and soon; and say, Amen.

May His great name be blessed forever and to all eternity.

Blessed and praised, glorified and exalted, extolled and honored, adored and lauded be the name of the Holy One, blessed be He, beyond all the blessings and hymns, praises and consolations that are ever spoken in the world; and say, Amen.

May there be abundant peace from heaven, and life, for us and for all Israel; and say, Amen.

A beam of light broke through the gray clouds and shone onto the gravesite. Rabbi Levi felt encouraged by this wondrous sight and continued the prayer with even more passion than before.

He who creates peace in His celestial heights, may He create peace for us and for all Israel; and say, Amen.

The gathering was heartened by the light and how it enhanced the colors and beauty of the grave. The marble headstone was a simple affair. It read "Johann Kraus" and beneath that, two words announced themselves to all who came by as an encapsulation of the man's life.

As Rabbi Levi finished the prayer, all looked at the now illuminated headstone. The words seemed to proclaim themselves to all there and to the entire world as well.

Good Prevails

Samuel Rosenberg
Webster, Massachusetts